Come By Here

Come By Here

OLIVIA COOLIDGE

Illustrated by Milton Johnson

Houghton Mifflin Company Boston

BOOKS BY OLIVIA COOLIDGE

CAESAR'S GALLIC WAR
CROMWELL'S HEAD
EGYPTIAN ADVENTURES
GEORGE BERNARD SHAW
GREEK MYTHS
THE KING OF MEN
LEGENDS OF THE NORTH
LIVES OF FAMOUS ROMANS
THE MAID OF ARTEMIS
MAKERS OF THE RED REVOLUTION
MARATHON LOOKS ON THE SEA
MEN OF ATHENS
PEOPLE IN PALESTINE
ROMAN PEOPLE
TALES OF THE CRUSADES
THE TROJAN WAR
WINSTON CHURCHILL
AND THE STORY OF TWO WORLD WARS
COME BY HERE

Table of Contents

Introduction

THIS STORY, based on a real adventure, gives a picture of the age when the Civil War was ancient history, but the movement for civil rights was equally far in the future. Black people lived in their own world, having only casual contacts with white people across whose path they happened to drift. Some kindly white people did offer Minty Lou a helping hand, but they were too indifferent to follow her back into her own world and see what happened to her there. Other white people, like Mrs. Murch and the piglike rent man, took shameless advantage of the poor and helpless.

Black people were hardly kinder to Minty Lou than white people. The bitter fight for survival made them selfish, while their narrow horizons meant lack of imagination. To them, the big city was a frightening place where people of any age dropped out of sight without anybody caring. It hardly occurred to them to worry about the fate of one little girl. Besides, black people did not write letters, talk on the telephone, or read the papers. Thus Minty Lou's neighbors had no way of knowing when Big Lou's funeral was unless Grandma told them. Mr. Prince found his way to where Grandma lived, but he may well have had some trouble in finding her address.

Baltimore Negroes were mostly up from the country, where their parents had got along by casual labor and were little removed from their old condition of slavery. Samuel Hayes was a hard worker, but he could not get a regular job. He raised a garden, killed and salted a couple of pigs in the fall, and traded eggs for petty cash when he was desperate. He chopped his firewood where farmers would let him have it for the clearing. His children went three or four years to school, half a grade a year; and it was an effort to buy them pencils and paper. One of these children was Big Lou.

Lou is an example of the ability lying untapped among Negro families. Unlike Helen Robbins, who was an able woman, too, she had made good. Luckily her generation did have basic education, and she had inherited a natural magnetism as well. No one liked Helen Robbins, but everybody loved Big Lou.

No doubt success had made her too ambitious, too eager to throw away her past, too anxious to adapt herself to a purely white world. All the same, she was in her way like Harriet Tubman, unwilling to put up with ignorance and degradation.

Lou's tragedy was that her success was an individual matter. Rooted in nothing, it could not when she died be handed on. The hospital did not even give her job to Edna. It found a white woman, even though it had to pay more.

Minty Lou had ability and a certain amount of luck, in that she survived. All the same, we can hardly suppose that her grandparents in Cambridge found her easy to bring up. She had learned too early in life that society is callous. Later she was able to see how much of this unkindness had been due to the cultural, economic, physical, and social division which existed between the black and white races, poisoning both.

Minty Lou never became a nurse. By studying along after school, she passed the eighth grade. Her children would go to high school, and the next generation to college. But Minty Lou grew up during an age in which black people lived and died in an obscurity which was almost total. Yet it is the characters formed in their battle, the abilities developed against their background which produced the black race as we know it today. It is right to look back on Minty Lou and to realize that she was going somewhere—not where she hoped, perhaps, but still somewhere. Obscure people have much to contribute which ought not to be forgotten, even though their actual names may not endure.

Come By Here

Monkey Man

MINTY LOU PAYSON was making her bed, which she was young enough to find complicated. She kept darting around to one side to twitch it straight, then going back to the other. Her old quilt, spread single because it was spring, was big and awkward. Minty Lou had her Saturday pinafore on, white with blue smocking and heavily starched, so that she had to be careful not to crumple it under the mattress as she tucked.

She plumped up her pillow and started to spread a white coverlet over the top. Her head, decorated with four white bows, bobbed energetically. At last she gave a final pat to an obstinate lump and stepped back to look, putting out her tongue between her open lips as she considered. There was nothing left to do but to take her white rugs off the chair where they lay folded and spread them over the painted boards. They had been given as a christening present to Minty Lou by a white lady for whom Momma had worked in the hospital kitchen. Then after a while the white lady had left; and Momma had been given her job, though for less money on account of having a second-grade education. The white rugs, symbol of the job as well as of the lady, had become a kind of mascot for the household. Momma said such pretty things ought to be looked after, but Poppa muttered that them rugs was lucky and hadn't ought to be stepped on. In any case, the first thing Minty Lou did when she went to her room was to take up her rugs; and as she went out again, she put them down. No foot ever trod on them, not even Minty Lou's own bare foot when the icebreakers were out in the bay, though she had no heat upstairs save what circulated from the stove in the living room below, which was only lit on Sundays.

"Minty Lou! Minty Lou!" called Momma from the kitchen, her big voice rolling through the house, charged with the energy that she put into everything. "Minty Lou! Listen!"

Minty Lou stopped with the rugs in her hand, cocking her head. She could hear a clop of hooves in the street and a clatter of wagon wheels going past, but that meant nothing special. One of the kids on the sidewalk had started to yell, and the new lady from next door came out onto the steps to scream at him. Presently the lady went back inside and a half silence fell in which more distant noises could be heard. Down the street echoed

a bawling cry, rising and falling with a hoarse
flourish on four notes . . . "Kni-ive-sO-O!"

"Monkey man!" screamed Minty Lou, dropping
the white rugs almost anyhow and tearing across
the landing and down the stairs. "Momma, monkey man!"

"Careful, careful!" Lou Payson came out of the kitchen in time to catch Minty Lou as she stumbled over the three bottom steps and very nearly fell into the dining room sideboard, on which stood a cut-glass bowl with wax apples in it and a couple of real oranges to look pretty. "You'll want some peanuts for the monkey. Wait a minute!"

She dodged back into the kitchen; and Minty Lou started jumping up and down, up and down, feet together, while she was waiting.

Momma came back with a little bag of peanuts. "There's a penny for the tune," she said. "Don't drop it! You can tell him to stop outside the door, and I'll have my knives ready."

"Kni-ive-sO-O!"

Minty Lou dashed out of the front door, leaving it swinging, and jumped down the last three steps into the street.

There were plenty of kids around the monkey man, who was just stopping down the block to grind a kitchen knife, ten cents paid in advance. He stood on the step of his cart, painted green with a faded red panel which said KNIFE GRINDER in black and yellow letters. His old brown horse had a white patch around one eye, which gave him a half-blind expression, and he was wearing a plaited straw hat drooping over his forehead. But nobody cared about the horse. The hurdy-gurdy was sitting up in the front of the cart, leaving room for the grindstone and for the knife cleaner, a round apparatus painted like a face with a handle in its mouth. It could clean six stained steel knives at once, the handles sticking out around its head like Minty Lou's pigtails — six knives for a nickel. Nobody looked at the knife cleaner, or even at the grindstone, though a shower of sparks flew as the grinder held the blade. People clustered around the hurdy-gurdy with its drum attachment, which towered up in the front of the cart facing onto the sidewalk. A hole had been cut through the panel saying KNIFE GRINDER, so that the owner could poke a handle through to play a tune.

The monkey was sitting on the front of the cart, attached to the hurdy-gurdy by a chain which ran to a belt around his waist. He was wearing a faded red coat and a red brimless cap which he took off and offered to the children, shuffling onto the shaft of the cart like a little old man with sad, sad eyes who could tell them a lot of things about being alone in a big city without monkey friends of his own, and without even knowing what sort of thing a monkey was when he was free. Some of the children put fingers in their mouths and stared back solemnly; but others were already jumping up and down, calling, "Monkey, monkey! Give us a tune!" Freddy Lane, who lived next door but two, walked all around the horse on his hands to show he could do it, waving his bare feet so close that the animal threw up his head and hitched at the cart.

"Whoa back!" yelled the grinder, jerking at the long reins which trailed behind the organ. He took his foot from the treadle for a moment and stood up.

"Give little Jimmy something in his hat, kids! Give Jimmy nuts and watch him eat 'em. Give him a penny, and he'll put it in his pocket. When he has five pennies there, I'll play you a tune." He set the treadle going again and bent over the grindstone.

Some of the kids put peanuts in the hat and watched the monkey eat them, mumbling them with his hand before his face in case somebody might snatch them back again. Freddy Lane put in a stone, and the monkey made a face and chattered at him. The kids laughed.

"Don't tease poor Jimmy!" said the monkey man, crossing the sidewalk to hand the knife back to its owner. "Don't cut your thumb on it, ma'am. Ten cents for an edge like it never had brand-new. Yes, ma'am, only ten cents for an edge on that big knife! Give Jimmy a penny for a tune!"

One of the kids dropped a penny into Jimmy's hat. He took it out and smelled it, making a funny face so that the children laughed. Then he put it into a pocket which was stitched onto his red coat. Someone else dropped a peanut on the ground, and Jimmy swung neatly down from the shaft of the cart to pick it up. He swung back up again and ate the peanut. Then he scratched himself under the arm.

"Only five pennies for a tune," urged the knife grinder. He looked around him, but did not see any more trade from the ladies hanging out of

upper windows or standing on the little flights of
steps, fresh whitened for Saturdays, which led to
their front doors. There were not many pennies
among these kids and too many peanuts. Already
Jimmy was stuffing nuts into his pocket for later
on.

"Kni-ive-sO-O!" When he flapped the reins on
the cart, the old horse moved at a walking pace up
the street with the children capering around him.

Minty Lou's penny was hot in her hand, but her
peanut bag was nearly empty. She went up the
street, skipping with every step, but avoiding the
cracks in the pavement because cracks were for
bad luck. "Momma, Momma!" shouted Minty
Lou. "Look, monkey!"

Lou Payson was out on the sidewalk ready with
three knives, a whole thirty cents' worth, laughing
all over her big face like a kid herself. "What,
didn't you give him your penny yet?" she asked,
pretending to shake her head. "You sure are on
the chintzy side, just like your pop!"

Minty Lou giggled because that was a joke.
She had saved up her penny for a tune outside
her own door where Momma could enjoy it . . .
which was just why Momma had brought out
three knives though they didn't need no edge. As
for Poppa, he was standing behind Momma in the
doorway, holding up a nickel between his finger
and thumb, a whole nickel! Chintzy! She put a
hand over her mouth to stop laughing.

Jimmy held out his hat to Minty Lou, who put her penny in it. The knife grinder whistled to him, and he ran across the drum on four legs and dropped onto the knife grinder. He put the penny into his master's hand and began to rummage in his pocket, stopping to smell what he brought out and now and then to eat a peanut.

"One, two, three!" counted the knife grinder. "Come on, Jimmy!" He rattled the chain, and Jimmy dropped a peanut to scrabble in his pocket. "Four!" said the knife grinder. "Sure you ain't got five, eh, Jimmy?" Jimmy turned his pocket inside out to show it was empty.

"All right, all right!" the knife grinder said. "Who'll give a penny for a tune? Only one more penny! What about it, kids?"

Freddy Lane gave a penny, and Poppa said, "Here's a nickel. Double time for the kids, eh? That's two nickels, mister."

The knife grinder held out one hand for Pop's nickel and the other for Momma's knives. He put the money in his pocket and the knives on the edge of the cart. Then he took out an old red handkerchief and mopped his forehead. "Ten cents for a tune and three knives to grind! Nah you-all talkin' business!" He looked around on the kids and screwed up one little blue eye in a wink. "C'mon, now! Whaddya want I give you first, them knives or the tune?"

"The tune, the tune!" All the kids shouted their

loudest, while Momma smiled and nodded her
head to show she agreed.

"OK. You-all said it." The knife grinder deliberately took off his waistcoat, folded it, and put it
down on the knife cleaner. He rolled his sleeves
up, rummaged for the handle, and carried it
around to fit into the hole. Then he took a hitch
at his trousers, spat into the gutter, and cocked an
eye at Jimmy, who had scrambled onto the tilt of
the cart. Glancing at his audience, which was by
now watching in tense silence, he put both hands
onto the handle and turned.

The hurdy-gurdy began to play . . . *kerplonk-
ety plonk* . . . "Put On Your Old Gray Bonnet!"
Jimmy shuffled into a dance like a poor old man
who knew he was not funny anymore. Some of the
kids began to sing, "With the blue ribbons on it,"
in shrill treble voices. The back of the knife
grinder swayed up and down.

Freddy Lane started a tap dance on the sidewalk, slapping his bare feet down heel and toe,
his face solemn, his arms and body hardly moving,
his feet twinkling in and out. Two or three of the
other kids were jigging in time.

The hurdy-gurdy changed to "Daisy, Daisy!"
Minty Lou and Mandy Hughes caught hands and
started swinging. Other kids were swinging one
another, first one way, then back again. The knife
grinder's shirt was sticking to his back. Jimmy
kept up his sad little shuffle on the cart.

"See Me Dance the Polka!" ground out the hurdy-gurdy. Pop put his arm around Momma's waist and they were away . . . one–two–three–hop! One–two–three–hop! *Boom!* went the drum and *Crash!* went the cymbals on top.

For all her bigness, Momma was light on her feet; and she dearly loved to dance. Around and around they went, swinging and dipping and bouncing, up the sidewalk, down the street and up again, just as if they were one person and not two. "See Me Dance the Polka!" Little boys and girls were trying the hops, while in the corner between the front steps and the wall, Freddy Lane went on tapping, heel, toe, heel, toe, his eyes on his pattering feet.

"Shut that noise!" That was Mr. Prince Morgan, the lodger on the third floor back, who was leaning out of Minty Lou's window to yell at the crowd. Mr. Prince was a waiter at the Pavilion, where on weekends the Merry Band played waltzes and polkas or the new ragtime tunes till four in the morning. Mr. Prince didn't get to bed till six on account of clearing up, so that on Saturday mornings he had to sleep. But who would have thought that a little music would have waked him?

Nobody took notice of Mr. Prince. The ladies on their steps were clapping their hands to the music, and younger couples had started to dance behind Momma and Pop. Mr. Prince pounded on the sill and shouted a cuss word or two at the knife grinder, who never looked up. People that had paid for double time were going to get double from him. He grunted to himself as the hurdy-gurdy came to the end of one performance and went back, *kerplunkety plunk,* to "Put On Your Old Gray Bonnet!"

"You . . . you!" yelled Mr. Prince. He put back his head inside the room, grabbed the first things he could find, and sent them sailing out of the window at the hurdy-gurdy.

Minty Lou's rugs came twisting down, one of them falling on the hindquarters of the old horse, who woke up with a jerk and started moving up the street, thinking that his master had flapped his reins. The other landed on the knife grinder, who dropped the handle, cutting off his tune with a half-finished *kerplunk!* He snatched the rug off his head and flung it in the gutter, rushing around to jerk the reins and "Whoa!" his horse.

Everybody stopped dancing and looked up. Mr. Prince had an audience for his cussing; and he made the best of it, yelling and shaking his fist.

People did not answer back because Mr. Prince was well respected on account of being on first-name terms with the Merry Band. But the knife grinder was not about to be cussed out by colored folk or to have rugs thrown at him right in the middle of doing what he'd been paid for. He shook his fist back at Mr. Prince and roared even louder, calling him all sorts of low Georgia names

and going so red and angry that most of the kids clumped together, scared by the storm.

"Nah, nah! What's all this here?" The cop came strolling down the street free and easy like he always did. "Hold on, George," he said to the knife grinder. "You'll burst a blood vessel! Besides, you can't make trouble on my beat, and you

know that. You, Joe, up there at the window, shut
your big mouth!"

Mr. Prince did shut his mouth because cop
trouble was sure enough going to lose him his job.
He banged the window down hard and went back
to bed.

George glared around, still looking for somebody to fight with; but nobody wanted to start
anything in front of the cop and the kids. When

no one met his eye, he snatched up Momma's three knives and threw them in the gutter. He took out her thirty cents and sent them tinkling over the sidewalk.

"Grind your own knives and be damned," he shouted, "you no-good niggers!" He flapped the reins on the horse's back and rumbled off with Jimmy crouched on the drum like a little bag of bones, his miserable face peering back at all the kids.

"That sure does mean bad luck!" said Poppa sadly. He picked up the knives and the change, shaking his head over each one of them. Momma rescued the rugs.

"It's all right," she told Minty Lou, who was staring after Jimmy with big, frightened eyes. "Never mind about your rugs, honey. I'll wash them out."

She held out a hand to Minty Lou, who took it without one word. They both went in. Other people drifted away, and a cloud came over the sun.

Custard Pie

GRANDMA PUT OUT HER PLATE for a second help. "I sure do love hog chitlins!"

"Better leave a little room, Ma," Jim Payson told her grinning. "There's pie."

"Pie!" yelled Grandma's Gordie, who was only a year older than his own niece, Minty Lou. He bounced in his seat. "J'hear that, kids? There's pie!" He kicked Bert, who was sitting next him, and Bert kicked back.

"Hush up, boys," ordered Grandma, cuffing Bert, who was nearest. "Anybody'd think you-all hadn't never ate pie."

"Never did eat none," Gordie retorted, kicking Bert again because he wouldn't dare kick back.

"Anybody'd think," continued Grandma, who never blamed her youngest for anything, "that you kids hadn't never sat at a dinin' table to home. Put that away, Tom!" Tom, who was the oldest and stupidest of her kids, shoved his new knife back into his pocket and grinned.

"Never did set at our dinin' table to home," persisted Gordie.

It was time to change the subject. Grandma's dining suite was the pride of her life, and she loved to pretend that she and the kids used it every weekend like Lou and Jim.

"Custard pie!" announced Lou with a great big grin which showed every tooth in her head. "Real eggs!"

"I rolled the crust! I rolled the crust!" cried Minty Lou.

For once Grandma didn't say what a big girl Minty Lou was getting and give her a kiss. Delight at the treat was fighting a battle with envy inside her. Envy won.

"My, my!" she said, her voice sharp. "Livin' high, ain't we?" She looked at her own swollen hands, crisscrossed with countless tiny scars from the oyster shucking. "Didn't never get too much time for bakin'," she said. "Done raised a proper family instead."

This time it was Jim's turn to smooth things over. Whenever his ma was annoyed, she started complaining because Lou had only the one child, and she a girl. That's what came of reading magazines and dancing to all hours and earning as much as your husband! Ma had always had it hard, and she thought that every woman should have it hard, too. She never understood how wonderful Lou was and how lucky an ignorant fellow like himself, fit only for a dirty job at Bethl'em Steel, was to have married her. All the same, good old Ma had her soft side. There was Gordie, and there was Minty Lou, who couldn't do wrong.

"So you helped Momma with the baking, did you?" he said to his daughter.

Minty Lou was used to being petted, and she liked to show off to Gordie and the kids. She told everybody how she had rolled the piecrust, dried the dishes for Momma, damped the ironing, and helped with the dusting, and all the other things she did on weekends.

Grandma smiled all over her face as she said what a big girl Minty Lou was getting, and she made her stand up back to back with Gordie. Everybody decided she was the taller, even if she was a whole year younger. Gordie pinched her, and when she yelled out, even Grandma told him to leave her alone. Poppa boasted that the first-grade teacher said Minty Lou was smart as a whip. She could already write her name as good as he did his own. Grandma said none of her kids didn't have much use for schooling, but Gordie was sharp enough when he wanted to be. Gordie put out his tongue at Minty Lou behind Grandma's back.

Momma got up to change the plates with Minty Lou to help her. They had not enough plates to go around twice, so they washed and dried them in the kitchen, while Pop explained to his ma how

the custard pie was special on account of the fresh
country eggs Lou's momma had sent up to her on
the boat from Cambridge. Grandma asked how
come Ar'minta Hayes wan't trading her fresh eggs
to the store for bread soda or molasses. You needn't
tell her those Hayeses had cash money to spare,
even if Ar'minta did work at the pea picking
along with all the poor trash in Cambridge. And
now she came to think of it, how come Ar'minta,
as couldn't read nor write, nor Sam'l neither, was
sending eggs to Baltimore? If Lou'd said oncet,
she'd said a hundred times how she couldn't never
get news of her ma and dad if it wan't from some
new feller that come to work at Bethl'em Steel,
fresh up from Cambridge.

Pop did not need to do any explaining because
Grandma did not really want to know. She liked
talking over Ar'minta Hayes, whom she despised
because she and Sam'l hadn't had the git-up-and-
go to move to Baltimore, where oyster shucking in
winter and canning in summer made up a regular
job. Why, a woman who still had three kids on
her hands could own a dining room suite and have
a parlor as well! Grandma had fought her way up
from a three room shack and a dug well with a
bucket on a rope. All she wanted to do was boast
about her victory.

Momma had ready a flat glass dish turned up at
the sides with bubbles around it which Pop had
bought for her birthday. She put the custard pie

on it and let Minty Lou carry it while she collected the plates. "Careful!" she said. "Don't tilt it now and slide it off!"

Minty Lou bit her lip, keeping her eyes on what she was carrying. The dining room was naturally dark because it lay between the front room and the lean-to kitchen at the back, which meant that it only had one narrow window where its back wall was a little wider than the kitchen. It was a small room and crowded with seven people. Grandma was still talking in the high voice which dominated her unruly family. Gordie was rocking back and forward, bringing the front legs of his chair down onto the floor with noisy thumps. Minty Lou threaded her way between the door to upstairs and the sideboard, moving slowly around Pop's chair, which was pushed back from the table. Tom was whistling a tune between his teeth.

There was all this noise going on, and then the door to the stairway was shut, which it never was unless they used the dining room. Minty Lou could not hear Mr. Prince Morgan coming down the stairs after having his Sunday sleep-in. The door stuck and opened suddenly as Mr. Prince pushed impatiently at it. It flew out against Minty Lou, sending pie and pie dish through the air to crash on the bare boards. Splinters of glass flew in every direction. Grandma screeched, and Lou came running.

Everybody was talking at once. Mr. Prince

was apologizing. Jim Payson was saying that it
was only an accident. Minty Lou was wailing.
Grandma was giving her opinion that a little dirt
didn't hurt for once and that parts of the pie could
be saved. Lou was pointing to the broken glass that

lay everywhere and saying she dassn't serve such a
mixture at her table. Gordie was uttering regular
groans which sounded like "Booh!" and Bert was
telling Tom how he might have knowed it when
they saw a walleyed dog on the way over. Never
was any luck around a walleye. If he could have
cotched that dog, he'd have tied a can to its tail
and given it a kick.

Lou said it couldn't be helped, and she had some
gingerbread which had come up from Cambridge
with the eggs. The boys brightened because gingerbread was sure better than nothing. Lou said that
Mr. Prince must stay and taste it because her own
momma made the chewiest gingerbread there ever
was and had packed it right careful in one of the
cookie tins they gave her at the store. Mr. Prince
said how he did love gingerbread ever since he
was a boy, and how he was sorry to be so clumsy,
and how he was a waiter himself and knew acci-
dents did happen. Then everybody said how it
didn't matter, and Mr. Prince said it did. He took
out a nickel from his pocket and held it out to
Minty Lou, who was still sobbing, and said she
should buy some licorice with it down to the store.

Minty Lou pushed his hand away and said,
"You dirtied my rugs and I hate you!" Then she
cried louder than ever.

Lou said that Minty Lou had better mind her
manners. The rugs was washed and no harm done.
Was she going to take that nickel like a good girl

and make her curtsy, or was she going upstairs
until she got over her temper?

Minty Lou went upstairs, leaving the door open,
and she cried and cried as loud as she could so that
everyone should hear her. She would not even take
up her rugs. She stamped on them, with the shoe
on her foot and all. They weren't clean, they
weren't! There had been horse dirt in that gutter,
and there was a stain on one Momma hadn't gotten
out. You could see it, you could! She stamped on
it again.

She couldn't go on crying all day, and she
wasn't sure that Momma would save any gingerbread if she didn't come down. Them boys
wouldn't leave her a crumb! Besides, she knew
she'd have to take that nickel and make her curtsy
to Mr. Prince sooner or later. She decided she'd
give all the licorice to the boys and sobbed again.

Presently she crept to the head of the stair to
find out if they were talking about her and if Mr.
Prince had gone. But Mr. Prince was still there,
and Momma was telling everybody the great news
which she had saved to go with the pie. There was
this brother of Mr. Prince's, who was a deckhand
on the steamboat *Joppa* that was on the Choptank
River run down Chesapeake Bay. Mr. Prince had
got him to inquire from the Cambridge jitneys
at the wharf and from farm carts coming down
to ship out produce and from the wagons picking
up store goods if anybody knew Sam'l and

Ar'minta Hayes. Pretty soon somebody did, and
Grandmomma Hayes had hitched a ride herself
in one of the jitneys and come down to the wharf
to meet the *Joppa* on her next run. Everybody was
well, and Allie was married, so that there was
only the two kids to home; but Grandpa's sister's
husband had got into debt running up stores on
the tick. He was in the jailhouse, so that there was
seven they had to help to keep as well as their own.

"Them Hayeses was always soft," Grandma said
with a little sniff.

Grandmomma Hayes was picking peas for the
farmers, and the kids would help with the beans
when school was out.

"She was always a good picker," said Lou,
remembering, "but we kids had to tote the basket
for her when it was full." You could hear she was
smiling by the way she said it. Minty Lou gave an
angry sob because Momma didn't seem to mind
what she was doing upstairs.

"Well, so then I sent her the fare," said
Momma, bursting with her news. "So that she's
coming up on the *Joppa* between the beans and the
tomatoes. School's out, and the kids can manage
for a week. Just fancy, my own momma that ain't
so much as seen Minty Lou and ain't never been off
the Choptank River in her born days! She can
have the third floor front! I didn't rent it till I
knew if she was coming. Momma ain't never had
a room to herself in her whole life!"

"I should say not!" agreed Grandma sharply. She shared her own bed with Gordie, while Bert and Tom had the other. Grandma did have two bedrooms, but there was her daughter Arlene and Arlene's husband too. She'd hinted and hinted that Arlene and Joe might like Lou's third floor front, but Lou was always deaf to what she didn't want to hear.

"It's a real holiday treat," said Lou happily in the rich, warm voice that made everybody feel good. Even Grandma allowed that she'd be glad to see Ar'minta and began planning to show off her dining room and parlor. She thought she might ask Ar'minta to dinner and was plunged in calculations about salt pork and greens, but it turned out that Lou had everything already planned.

"I saved up my days off," she said in triumph. "And it's Minty Lou's birthday the next week, so I promised we'd have the party while her grandma's here. It's on the Saturday, and you're all invited." She looked around her. "You, too, Mr. Prince," she added cheerfully.

Minty Lou was halfway down the stairs, but she stopped and would not go another step. She did not like Mr. Prince. She hated him. He tickled her neck when they met on the stairs, and he called her "Min" because he said she was too small for a big name. Mr. Prince was pure bad luck, but Momma was so happy about Grandmomma com-

ing up from Cambridge that she wouldn't see it.
She said she didn't like those silly notions that
Minty Lou was picking up from the kids in school.
She'd better pay more attention to Sunday school,
where they didn't say nothing about ghosts, nor
devils in the closet, nor sticking pins in the ground
to make it rain. Minty Lou crouched on the stairs
and heard Mr. Prince say Saturdays was his big
day at the Pavilion, but that Momma was welcome
to borrow his victrola with the great big horn and
the picture on it of a black-and-white dog listening
to the music.

"Did you hear that, Minty Lou?" asked Lou
without raising her voice. "Now isn't that something? Hadn't you better come and thank Mr.
Prince like a good girl?"

It really was something, so that Minty Lou
came down a little shyly and said, "Thank you,
Mr. Prince," and took the nickel and made her
curtsy — one foot behind the other and bob.

Mr. Prince said, "You and I are friends, Min,
ain't we?" and he tickled her neck.

Minty Lou did not say yes, and she did not say
no. She ran to her momma and buried her face on
her shoulder.

So everything was all right. Minty Lou ate her
gingerbread, and then she went down with the kids
to the store, which was open on Sundays. She
bought three peppermint canes and two long sticks
of licorice and gave them all to the boys. Tom

looked at her in his slow way and said, "Don't you want no candy? You sick to your stomach?"

Gordie grabbed his share and said, "So she don't want none. So ain't that just too bad? If you don't like it, Tom, just give it to me." He snatched a bit out of Tom's clumsy fingers and crammed it into his mouth. Tom cuffed him, while Gordie kicked his shins and screamed that he'd tell Grandma. Nobody bothered any more about Minty Lou.

Grandma Minty

MINTY LOU stood on one foot while she scraped
a dusty shoe down her white cotton stocking. She
had her best starched petticoat on, which sure did
prickle in this hot sun. But while she wriggled,
she never once stopped talking. She had hundreds
of questions to ask because the waterfront district
was crowded with wagons drawn by huge cart
horses, loaded donkey carts, a noisy truck or two,
people of all sorts furiously moving things about.
Over all hung smells of tar, fish, and tobacco.

"What's our ship doing with her big wheel?"
screamed Minty Lou above the noise, pointing at
the incoming *Joppa,* whose near paddle wheel had
started reversing to swing her around.

"If you wait and watch," said Momma pa-
tiently, "you'll see."

"What's that man standing on the end for?"

"To throw a rope."

"Where's my grandmomma?"

"Colored folks is at the back where the cargo comes off. They has to wait until the gangway is clear."

"What's a gangway?"

"Hush up and watch," Momma said. "You don't hear this lady yelling into my ear, do you? She minds her manners."

The lady next to Momma mopped a broad face and beamed, remarking that the little girl was a cute kid, and that it sure was hot in the sun, and that she had four of her own, but quieter like. Her feet were swelled with standing so that her shoes hurt, and she was waiting for her sister's boy, who was coming from Golden Hill (a real country kid) to work in the city because her sister . . . She flowed on, smothering even Minty Lou in a froth of talk which seemed to have been bottled up inside her until Momma's remark had pulled out her cork.

Luckily the gangways were soon going out. Waiting white folk began to press forward while colored drew back from the rear gangway, down which baskets of crabs packed in wet weeds, boxes of beans for the market, and huge barrels stenciled with mysterious letters came trundling out on porters' dollies piled so high that you could hardly see who wheeled them. One of these loads stopped opposite just long enough for a short, stout man to yell to Momma, "You Mis' Hayes' daughter, eh? She's a-coming. Got a baby with her."

"Mr. Morgan," screamed Lou in return, "did you say *baby?*"

A frightened steer, pulled onto the gangway by two ropes, bolted down it at Mr. Prince Morgan's brother, who hitched up his dolly and got out of the way in a hurry.

"He didn't say *baby,*" Lou protested to the lady, who was still talking. "He couldn't have said *baby.* Momma wouldn't . . . " Her voice trailed off in a funny way as though she could not be quite certain what her momma would . . . The lady did not even interrupt what she was saying.

There were a lot of steers in this consignment, so that Mr. Morgan and the rest were far too busy getting them ashore to bother about questions; while the second-class passengers, which meant the colored section, had to stand out of the way where nobody could see them. However, at last they began to come ashore: a couple of sharp-looking men with tight collars and flashy ties, a few kids in country clothing, a whole family loaded down with boxes and bundles, and several women in long, tight skirts and fancy hats up for a visit.

"Is that my grandmomma? Is that my grand-momma?" screamed Minty Lou, pointing at one after another.

Lou only shook her head. She was peering up the gangway with an expression more worried than welcoming. "Baby!" she muttered.

When Grandmomma did appear at the top of

the gangway, she could not possibly have been anybody else. She was only about five feet high, and
her clean cotton dress was shabby. She had a
handkerchief on her head like a field hand and
carried a bundle neatly wrapped in an old tablecloth. But in her free arm, she certainly did have
a baby.

Lou rushed forward and lifted her right off her
feet in a big hug, baby and all.

"My great girl!" Grandmomma exclaimed.
"Nobody ain't done that to me since you went to
Baltimore along of Jim." She chuckled. "Allie
ain't no bigger'n me by so much as an inch."

"But what's that baby?"

"First things first," Grandmomma retorted.
"You was always a one for burstin' out. This here's
Josepheen." She nodded her head at a clumsy girl
in country clothes who was half carrying, half
dragging a couple of grocery boxes down the gangway. "Come to Baltimore after her husband that
run off and left her. Ain't got no place to go." She
winked and lowered her voice. "Nor ain't right
likely to have if you ask me. I told her she could
share my bed; and the baby here, that's Arthureen
after her father, can go in a grocery box. Won't
be no trouble."

"Oh, Momma! And I had it planned for you to
have a room of your own all nice and clean."

"Ain't never slept single in my whole life,"
Grandmomma said with crisp decision, "let alone

in an empty room. Nor I wouldn't sleep easy
thinking of that poor thing on the streets. I doubt
she isn't right bright, but she's a good gal and
willing to work. It wasn't just her luck that I met
up with her. There was God in it!" She turned
away from her daughter with a little nod as though
this settled the matter.

"I might have known it," Lou said, shaking her
head sadly. "Isn't any use making plans when
you're around, but just once I wanted . . ." Her
voice died away because Grandmomma wasn't
even listening. She had put down her bundle to
beckon with her free hand at Josepheen.

"Come here, Josepheen, and meet my daughter.
It's all right."

Josepheen smiled shyly, but she did not look at
Lou — just rolled her eyes in a frightened way at
the wharf and the people as though she had never
dreamed that Baltimore was different from her
hometown with one wharf for the crab boats and
a steamer calling there three times a week.

Lou looked at Josepheen with her lips pursed,
but she said, "You're surely welcome."

Josepheen said, "Thank you, ma'am," bobbing
her head as though to a white lady, but she continued to look at the dockside, probably expecting
that everyone in town had come to meet the *Joppa,*
including her Arthur.

Minty Lou tugged impatiently at her momma's
hand. She didn't see why anyone should make a

fuss about Josepheen and her baby when they did
not so much as notice her at all. "That's *my*
grandmomma!" she said loudly.

Lou gave herself a little shake. "Bless me! Here
we stand talking and you haven't so much as said

hello to your granddaughter that has your own
name, for all she's going to be a great big clumsy
girl like me."

She put an arm around Minty Lou's shoulders
to draw her forward, and Grandmomma smiled
at her all over her face. Minty Lou would not
give her a kiss because she was angry. She put out
a hand, as she had been taught to do with strangers,
and dropped a curtsy as she said, "Howdy do?"

"Minty Lou!" cried Momma, outraged; but
Grandmomma put back her head and laughed.

"Why, here's a little Baltimore lady! I ain't
Grandmomma, honey. That's too fine and fancy
for me. You'd best call me Grandma."

"I got a grandma," retorted Minty Lou, sulky
at being laughed at.

"Why, so you have, and I forgot about her!
Now ain't that just too bad! Well now, honey, you
and me has the same name. Why don't you call me
Grandma Minty? Did you know I've got a little
girl isn't three years over your age?"

Minty Lou said, "Yes," smiling just a little as
she let Grandma Minty give her a hug. She still
felt shy, but when they got on the streetcar, there
was room to sit down for once in the colored
section. Lou sat in back with Josepheen, and Minty
Lou sat ahead with Grandma Minty. Then it
turned out Grandma Minty had never ridden in a
streetcar, and she had never seen the iron hitching
posts with horses' heads outside the rich men's

houses, nor the Indian outside the cigar store, nor a private automobile, except now and then. Minty Lou had to point out everything, and Grandma Minty said she was having the best time. They laughed together about the posters outside the movie palace, which had a clown on them, and about a little dog which charged down on a big one and snatched away his bone. They sat together hand in hand and played a game to see which one of them could see the biggest number of red objects.

It was the beginning of the week, so that the iceman had just put in fresh ice; and Lou had got up early to fix a cold lunch before they went out. But Grandma Minty said she couldn't eat a bite. All she and Josepheen wanted was a lay-down after sitting up all night on a hard wooden bench. There were bunks in the *Joppa,* but Mr. Prince's brother had warned her they were full of chinches, and she hadn't wanted to get those critters in her clothes. Behind her hand she added to Momma in a whisper that Josepheen was on the edge of tears because she had not thought Baltimore was so big and she was wondering how she would ever find her Arthur in it. Better let her go upstairs and change the baby, which it was high time she did.

Momma and Minty Lou ate the lunch together after Momma had found Josepheen a pail for diaper-washing and showed her a line in the back yard and given her a piece of an old sheet that

she'd been saving for a duster. Lou did not eat too
much, and every so often she shrugged her shoulders or shook her head while Minty Lou chattered
on about what she had said and done with
Grandma Minty.

In about two days, everything was topsy-turvy.
The bathroom smelled of diapers, and Josepheen
had tearfully agreed that while Jim made inquiries
among the men at Bethl'em, she had better get
a job. Lou, vowing and declaring that she had
promised to recommend someone else, had gone to
the hospital and found Josepheen a job as cleaning
woman. Miss Purley, the hunchback down the
street who did baby-minding, had made room for
Arthureen, shaking her head and saying she didn't
ought to, considering how she had turned away
two other ladies. "She can't pay much rent," said
Grandma, clearly taking for granted that Josepheen would stay on in the third floor front for
good. "But then you know, Lou, you don't actually
need money."

Lou did not argue that, though she had promised Minty Lou a new party dress if she could
afford it. Jim did not say anything, as usual; but
he came behind Grandma Minty and gave her a
hug for no special reason except that she was
different from his ma.

That was the thing about Grandma Minty. She
was different, and everything around her seemed to
get different as well. When it came to Minty Lou's

birthday, for instance, Grandma Minty had never
so much as frosted a cake. Never had enough
sugar, she said; but she had the greatest fun
helping Lou to color bits of icing pink or blue and
watching while Lou squeezed them out of a bag
to write "Happy Birthday!"

"Never did learn my letters," she remarked
quite cheerfully to Minty Lou. "I was born into
slavery. Did you know that?"

Minty Lou stared at her wide-eyed. She knew
exactly what was meant because slavery was something every kid had learned about, even if older
people did not come out and discuss it. Grownups
never boasted about having been slaves, and if they
could not read "Happy Birthday" written in
frosting, they kept this to themselves. Even Poppa
practiced his writing with Momma in the evenings
and was shy about it if Minty Lou came down in
her nightgown into the kitchen. Grandma Minty
was the first person Minty Lou had ever known
who up and said outright she was born a slave, so
that she ought to be different for that reason . . .
not different the way she was, but more like Josepheen. Soon they licked the mixing bowl together,
turn and turn about, so that the subject was forgotten.

It came up again after the birthday party, once
more because Grandma Minty could never be
quite like anyone else. That was partly a grown-up
party because of Grandma Payson and her kids,

including Arlene, who was nearly seventeen, and her Joe, who washed dishes in a restaurant. The rest were kids like Freddy Lane, who were neighbors, or some of the girls in Minty Lou's class. Momma had bought the party dress after all, and Grandma Minty had brought up a pinafore in her bundle made out of a dress which a white lady had given her to cut up. It had washed out beautifully and was the prettiest pink trimmed with some lace out of the petticoat that had come with it. Grandma Payson had given her hair ribbons to match.

All the kids had brought presents like candy sticks and jacks and cutout dolls from glossy magazines, which were all the craze in school. Lou gave everyone a paper cap and whistle, the long kind that unrolled. When they were tired of prancing about and making noise, they had hide-and-seek and hunt-the-slipper. When they were tired of that, Lou brought the victrola belonging to Mr. Prince out into the back yard where the garbage cans had been cleared away for the party. Then the grownups hummed the tunes along, while the kids danced. Even Gordie danced, though he did not go to the same school or know the kids.

Mr. Prince's victrola made the party because voice boxes were not too common; and even if they had been, the records came expensive. But dancing around was hot, and it got time for re-

freshments. Lou brought out pop and ice cream
onto a card table set up in the shade of the next-
door house, while Grandma Minty went into the
kitchen for the cake.

She came out in a minute and stood outside the
doorway, holding it up in both hands with the
candles lighted. But just as everybody was taking
a breath for "Happy birthday to you!" Grandma
Minty opened her mouth and began to sing. She
had a fine rich voice, rounder than Momma's,
which rolled around the yard and floated up to
the windows of the ladies watching the fun from
next-door houses. But what Grandma Minty sang
was not "Happy Birthday." She sang,

> Get on board, li'l chillun,
> Get on board, li'l chillun,
> Get on board, li'l chillun,
> There's room for many a mo'.

Pretty soon one of the ladies began answering,

> I hear de train a-comin',
> A-comin' roun' de ben'.
> I hear de whistle blowin'
> To take us home agen.

Then everybody joined in the chorus,

> Get on board, li'l chillun,
> Get on board, li'l chillun,
> Get on board, li'l chillun,
> There's room for many a mo'.

It was rich and splendid, but it was not "Happy Birthday." Minty Lou in her party dress and her pink ribbons did not feel the center of the song at all. Lou did start up "Happy Birthday" afterward, but it sounded silly and flat. Gordie put out his tongue at Minty Lou instead of singing, while she made a face back because nobody but Gordie was really looking at the birthday girl. Some of the ladies even called out to Grandma to sing again, but Grandma Payson called back that the kids liked the victrola better. Lou said it was time to go home when the cake was eaten.

When things start to go wrong, they generally stay that way. Grandma Payson and her kids stopped to supper, and Grandma spent the evening telling Grandma Minty about her dining room suite and how her kids were going to schools that did a whole grade in a year instead of half. She called Gordie to show off, but he was playing jacks with Bert and would not come. Lou had Minty Lou read a story instead. She did it without a mistake, and both grandmothers praised her; but pretty soon Grandma Payson had to tell how Gordie was a whole grade further ahead. Minty Lou did not get to say much, and she felt this specially when her momma said she was tired and ought to go early to bed.

"I'm a whole year older," she protested.

Grandma Payson laughed at that and petted

her a bit, but everything was spoiled. She went to
bed thinking how she would have to thank Mr.
Prince for the victrola, and he would tickle her
neck.

Allie's Tale

"WHY DID YOU SING that song instead of 'Happy Birthday'?" demanded Minty Lou next evening.

Grandma Minty looked surprised. "Why, honey, ain't that what we always sing . . . ?" She looked a question at Momma.

Lou was mending socks, and she didn't look up. She said, "Well, kids is different today, and that's good. Minty Lou isn't going to stop at no second grade, and she has to learn what white folks know, like them tunes on the victrola."

"Well, but don't she know her own folks? You can learn to talk good and have them that works under you call you Louisa instead of just plain Lou. But you got folks. You know who you is."

"That's just the trouble, Ma. I know who I am."

"So Minty Lou's to be like a little dog that somebody's trained to dance on his hind legs to music. He can look right smart, but what's the good to him if he don't know he's a dog and not a man?"

Lou took the sock off her darning egg and laid it aside. "I don't know but what you're right about the dog," she admitted. "There was a monkey come by here two, three weeks back. Remember him, Minty Lou?"

"He had a red coat," Minty Lou agreed, "and we put peanuts in his hat."

"Somehow or other," Lou said, "I never did see anything sadder than that monkey."

"And Mr. Prince threw my rugs out of the window and dirtied them all up. Mr. Prince is bad luck."

"Now hush your nonsense," Lou said. "Didn't Mr. Prince lend you the victrola, and aren't the rugs cleaned up? Let me tell you, Minty Lou, I'm tired of the ideas you're picking up from ignorant kids. If you haven't got something better to say, you'd best keep quiet."

"He tickled my neck," muttered Minty Lou sulkily.

Lou took no notice of this because she did not want to send Minty Lou to her room. She turned back to Grandma Minty. "Who are our folks, Ma? I know my own grandma, but you don't even know yours. My Grandma Allie was sold when she was six years old and don't so much as remember where she come from, let alone who her mother was. She didn't need folks." She put her hand down another sock and spread her fingers to look at the hole.

"She needed them bad," Grandma Minty retorted. "Do you think it was easy for her to learn how to go on with nobody caring, except how she did her work?"

"Is that your momma?" Minty Lou inquired. "What's she called? Is she very old?"

Grandma Minty put down the cloth with which she was polishing knives and looked across the room at her daughter. Lou said nothing.

"Is she very old?" repeated Minty Lou, who never liked not being answered.

Jim Payson put down the glass of beer which he was enjoying with his coat off and collar unbuttoned, and for once broke into the conversation. He said in his slow way, "Your mom was right, Lou. That was a sick monkey."

"Is she very old?"

Grandma Minty smiled and said, "Yes, she's got a lot of age onto her, has my ma. Can you count to a hundred?"

"Of course I can. I can count to a million if I want to."

"Well, my ma's nearly a hundred years old as far as she can tell. That's a lot of age."

Minty Lou nodded, impressed. "Does she have white hair? Is she really your momma?"

"She has white hair, but she's still spry. Yes, she's my ma, who gave me my name Ar'minta after Mis' Tubman."

"Who's Mis' Tubman?"

Grandma Minty raised her hands from her
work again. "You ain't never heard of Harriet
Tubman, honey? Not Harriet Tubman who gave
us our name, you and me both? Now that's too
bad, Lou."

Lou shook her head. "That was your name I
gave her and nobody else's. But it's your story;
and if you want to tell it to Minty Lou, you'd
best go ahead. There was never no keeping to any
sort of rule with you around."

Grandma Minty washed her hands in the kitchen
sink and put the knives in the drawer before fetching a pile of mending. She turned the lamp down
to stop it from smoking and threaded her needle
right up against it. She was not going to start until
she felt ready because storytelling was a thing she
aimed to do right. She did not need to know her
letters for that.

Grandma Minty's ma, she said, was called Allie,
like Momma's own sister down in Cambridge. No,
Allie didn't have no longer name; and she grew
up on a plantation down Church Creek way without knowing where she come from. When she was
fifteen year old, Master gave her to Buck, who was
servant to the overseer and helped work the field
gang. Buck was an easygoing man who didn't
never use the stick before he had to, so that he
was well liked among the people. Allie was respected, too, because she was a house servant and
worked in the kitchen. They got along fine, and

there was two boys born; and then there was two more that died of a fever that broke out in the cabins one year. Allie had that fever, too; and she was right sick, so that there was no more kids for a time. Then there was Jane, who was about four year old when it all happened.

It come about because young Master broke his neck racing. Crazy for horses he was and always ready to take a dare. Old Master never held up his head after that; and he died two year later, so that the plantation come to Miss Lucy that was married to a lawyer in Baltimore and had no use for it.

All the slaves was sold, even the old ones that nobody didn't much want, and the kids. There was a man come from down South looked them over for likely fellers to work in the big gangs on the cotton plantations. He picked out Buck first off, and Allie's boys as well, that was twelve and fourteen year old by now and handy with horses. But Allie, she was a house slave and still breeding, so that there was a-many wanted her. Old Missus favored good homes for her house servants, and she sold Allie with Jane to Mr. Clarke that was a boat builder living right in Cambridge.

They was very good to Allie at Clarkes'; and when she couldn't do nothing but cry that whole first week, they give her a pass to go and say good-by to Buck and her boys, that was being kept in the jailhouse for safety while the man that bought

them drove about buying up more slaves all over
the county.

She never could tell how they said good-by for
crying over it, but she went right early in the day
and come away early because the jailkeeper soon
put her out. But she couldn't seem to go back
where she belonged without her menfolk. She just
set down against the wall of the little old jailhouse
with her feet in the gutter and cried for a long
time.

There was a good many went by and didn't pay
no mind. White folks was used to them scenes,
and you'd better believe that the colored didn't
want no more trouble than they had. But after so
long, someone put a hand on Allie's shoulder.
When she looked up, there was a colored woman
with big broad shoulders and a sack of melons on
her back. She didn't say she was sorry for Allie,
nor that she'd see Buck and the boys in Heaven,
nor none of the things people tell you without
meaning. She just put her face down close to Allie's
ear and said to her quick and fierce, "Afore I'd let
them do that to me, I'd run off. That I would."
Then she hitched up her sack and walked away.

Allie was so surprised that she got to her feet
and looked after the woman, who was clumpsing
away under the heavy sack, looking just about as
broad as she was tall. A colored boy come by just
then, and Allie grabbed him. "Who's that there?"

He giggled a little, and he said, "That's only

Minty that's married to that no-good feller Jack
Tubman. She ain't nothing but a field hand, 'cept
that they sends her round town peddlin' fruit when
there's some ripe. She's crazy!" He wriggled out
of Allie's grip and ran away, not wanting to lounge
around in the open street where white folks could
see him.

"And was that Harriet Tubman?" Minty Lou
wanted to know. "How come she was Minty?"

"I never did know," Grandma Minty said, "if
her name was Ar'minta Harriet, which wan't too
likely in them days, or whether she tuk herself a
new name when she come North. But that's who
it was."

"And was that all she did?" Minty Lou was a
little disappointed.

Grandma Minty laughed. "Just like your ma,
always looking for to know the end afore the
beginning! You listen along."

Allie went back where she belonged to cook the
dinner, but there was tears in the soup that night
and for many nights after. Still, Clarkes was kind
to her and took a fancy to little Jane, so that after
a while she did cheer up, except when her new
master was after her to marry again and have more
children. Then she said she didn't want no more
if she was to be parted from them, and she cried
until he left her alone for a bit.

About the next spring, a colored man come to
the door with cheeses for the kitchen; and as he

handed them over, he spoke out of the corner of his mouth in a way that folks used to do when they didn't know who might be listening. He said right quick and quiet, "That crazy Minty's done run off. Got the dogs out arter her."

Allie didn't sleep that night for thinking of it. There's marshes round about Cambridge where a runaway might hide to be bitten by skeeters and sheep flies a day or two. But there ain't no food to be got where the dogs can't find you, nor no dry patch of land, nor no shelter from the rain that was coming down on the roof over Allie. Pretty soon it just naturally looked better to be whipped half to death and sold down South for running off.

Next day, the yard boy clipping hedges come round to the kitchen door for a cup of coffee left over from the family breakfast, and he whispered to Allie in the same sly way, "Ain't cotched her yet."

All the indoor servants listened to what was said by their white folks. There wasn't hardly a time when the door to the parlor didn't have somebody's ear pressed close to the keyhole. The upstairs servants knew places where the sound come up the chimney, or cracks in the floorboards where you could hear if you laid down. Soon it was Allie as was whispering to folk that come to the door how there was a reward put up for Minty Tubman, and slave catchers was hired to bring her in.

Most every day for a long time there was more
news. They'd cotched Minty in Chestertown. The
dogs had chased her acrost a Delaware swamp and
killed her there. She'd stole a rowboat Cornersville
way and was going for Baltimore, hiding in creeks
by day and rowing all night. Somebody seen her
driving a cart through Dover, cool as you please.
She'd been hiding with a free nigger in Baltimore;
but when they come for her, she shinnied out of
the back window and run off. Most people allowed
she was dead in the swamp, pointing out how there
weren't no buzzards left around over Cambridge,
or not so many as usual for that reason.

Nobody knew true from false, except that Minty
Tubman wan't seen around town anymore and that
the little old poster put up outside the jailhouse
was growing yellow and beginning to peel off. But
after so long, another story began to spread among
folks that nobody didn't know where it come from.
Harriet Tubman, that used to be called Minty,
was free up North. There wan't nobody else had
ever gotten clear away from Cambridge that
people knew of. Harriet's folks, who was still with
their old master, got whispered about in town
because they was kin, not to crazy Minty anymore,
but to brave Harriet Tubman.

A lot more time went by, and Allie's master
gave her to his yardman, who was known around
town as Clarke's Bob. But he made her a promise
that he wouldn't sell her children away from her

if she had any. Only for a long while she had none, she couldn't say why.

A good stretch after that, Clarke's Bob was sent out with a letter to a friend of the Missus downtown and wait for an answer. So he was coming along about the edge o' dark, at the time when colored folks had best get off the street pretty quick, or the patrollers'd catch 'em. Bob wan't hurrying much, being lame ever since a log dropped on his foot nigh on ten year back. And then Clarkes lived close by, so that he figured he had time. But others was scuttering along pretty quick, including an old lady with a big sunbonnet on and a hen in her arms, all scrunched down till she looked as broad as she was tall. Bob didn't seem to notice her much, but suddenly a voice spoke right up in his head, just as if there was somebody talking. And it said, "That there's Harriet Tubman!"

Bob stopped right in his tracks and looked around. Nobody wasn't paying no mind, unless it was a colored man across the street that was whistling to himself gentle and slow one of the tunes that our folk sing. He was watching Harriet Tubman go down that street, bold as brass, with nothing but a floppy sunbonnet to hide her face.

Harriet was hurrying all right, making for the corner and keeping her eyes on the ground in front of her feet. But afore she got to it, who should come a-strolling around it but Mr. Marshall that was Harriet's owner, that knew her since she was born and put up the reward for her, dead or alive. They wasn't more than a few yards apart, but she didn't see him.

The feller across the road stopped whistling, just cut off his tune in the middle of a note; and it seemed like a warning. Harriet hunched over a bit more, and that little old hen that had been sitting nice and peaceful in her arms, just clucking a little, gave a great squawk as though she'd been pinched and fluttered off across the road. Harriet went plundering after; and Mr. Marshall, that wasn't about to catch hens for an old colored woman, strolled down the street past Bob without ever knowing what sort of a chance he'd missed and how much it would cost him.

That cost Mr. Marshall plenty right away, because next morning Harriet's brothers and their women and kids was all gone off. It wan't no use getting out the dogs nor putting up posters nor paying slave catchers to get them back. Harriet knew the swamps like her own hand, and it was whispered there was white folks as didn't like slavery that was helping her smuggle poor people North to freedom. Down in Cambridge, a story was going around from back door to back door, whispered around the wharf, and passed from one gang to another across the fields. Pretty soon everybody heard how Harriet Tubman had swore she'd never rest till all her people as wanted to be free was safe up North.

You'd be surprised, honey, how news got around
in Cambridge and all the country about, into
places where folk didn't never go off the plantation
in their born days. Sometimes it was whispered.
Sometimes it was sung to the old tunes. Sometimes
it was told by the hoeing being done different at

the edge of the field where two plantations met. But however it was told, it all said the same. Them that wanted freedom must give a special sign; and sooner or later Harriet Tubman would lead them through the marshes, North by ways she knew.

There wan't so many as wanted to take that risk. Everybody knew how the marshes wan't no easy place to walk through. Most people that tried to escape always got caught; and you'd better believe the more people Harriet tuk off, the more the patrollers was on the lookout for her. Folks was frightened. They knowed what they was a-running from; but they didn't know freedom, and they was scared of that, too. But there was some that went, and there was a-many that didn't go theirselves but helped others to freedom by passing on the word, though it'd cost jail and a flogging if they was cotched out of their cabins after dark.

Allie didn't want for to run off. For one thing, she had a child coming. Then Bob, being lame, couldn't go along. Little Janey, that was the parlor-maid already, was sweet on a feller that worked in Clarkes' boatyard. Allie was fond of the Clarkes and they of her, so that she didn't want for to be free, but to stay with her folks.

Along about now, there was a steamboat put on the Choptank River for the run to Baltimore, just like the *Joppa*. Mr. Clarke, he had a big share in her and aimed for to make a heap of money. But

one day she cotched fire and burned to the edge
of the water, so that there was some lives lost, both
white and colored. The Clarkes was real upset,
and everybody allowed it was a terrible thing and
steamboats was risky. The very next week when
Janey was a-listening with her ear to the parlor
door, she heard the Master and Missus talking
together about all the money he'd lost with that
little old steamboat and how they'd have to sell
some of their slaves to pay up.

The Missus says they ought for to sell Janey,
that was nigh on twelve year old and worth a lot.
But the Master told as how he'd promised he'd
never sell Allie's children away from her. He
could see now he hadn't ought to have said it, but
he was a man of his word, he says, even when he
give it to his own slave. He stuck to that; and they
argued it up and down with him saying that he
could pay if he had time, but that somebody was
pressing him for money. At last the Missus says
to him, "Well, why don't we sell Allie? I don't
know what I'll do without her," she says, "but you
never promised you wouldn't sell Allie away, only
just her children."

Mr. Clarke says that was a good idea, and they
spent a while talking over how they wouldn't tell
Allie afore the baby was born in case she did herself harm.

When Janey come down into the kitchen to her
mother, Allie went stiff inside; and all the old

troubles that she'd been through come rushing
over her. Then she says, "I'm going. I'm going
off with Harriet Tubman. If I can walk or not,
I'm going. And if my baby's born in the mud of
the swamp and we both die there, I'm still going."

Janey agreed to run off, too, because she saw
there'd be no reason why they wouldn't sell her
instead if Allie'd gone. Bob says as how he couldn't
manage with his bad leg. Even when they told him
how Harriet had carried off her own father and
mother that couldn't walk no better than him, he
still says no. He wouldn't feel right to hold them
back, he says.

By now there was ways of knowing when Harriet Tubman was going to sneak back down South
and ways of telling who wanted to go with her to
freedom. Clarkes had their slave cabins down
near the end of their land at the back of the house.
There was a fireplace there where they cooked
beans or grits in a big pot, that is, in summertime
when cabins was hot. They used to set around that
and sing sometimes; and Clarkes allowed it, so
long as they didn't make too much noise. So that
evenin' they all set around and carried on the usual
way. But afore the fire burned low, Allie and Janey
moves out front where they could be seen in the
firelight; and they sung slow and careful like this.
Grandma Minty's voice rolled out, rich as cream,

> Cum by yere, Lawd,
> Cum by yere.

Oh, Lawd,
Cum by yere.

So then either one of the others'd make up
verses, some glad and then sorry. Then Allie and
Janey'd sing it again, always low and sad. They'd
look around them as though for something, but
nobody come.

Next night they carried on that way again, and
the next night after, and for a whole week after
that. It wan't never easy for them that did the
scouting for Harriet Tubman to get about. Some
was cotched doing it and flogged, but they never
let on. Allie didn't sleep nights for fear her child'd
be born early and they'd sell her away down South
afore Harriet come.

Along around the tenth night as they was a-sing-
ing, "Cum by yere, Lawd," and there was tears in
Allie's voice, they heard a little rattlin' noise at
the end of the lot. So they looked down thataway,
and in the moonlight, even though there wan't no
wind, they see them bushes shake.

Well, there wan't no more to be done but wait
for a word. Allie slept easy, and she went about
her work humming, "Cum by yere, Lawd," to
herself. Only while she was a-doing that, Janey
come down from the parlor to say how Mr. Clarke
was telling Missus that he got time to pay his debts
after all. Missus was saying she hadn't known how
she could get on without Allie and that she didn't
ever want to part with her.

"Whatever did Allie do?" asked Minty Lou enthralled.

She went out to sing again that same evening; only they sung, "I Got Shoes . . ." That's a happy tune, honey, and they sung it extra bright, so as to say they was happy where they was and Allie didn't need for to be parted from Bob, nor from Janey, nor the baby. They didn't never see no bushes shake; but they never got no word from Harriet Tubman, so they knowed the message got through.

Right after that the baby was born, and it was a girl. Allie wanted to call her Harriet, but she dassn't, seeing how Harriet stole nigh three hundred folk away from round Cambridge. So she remembered how Harriet's name used to be Minty, and she made up a story about how it come to her that her own mother's name was Ar'minta. "So that's how I come to be called Ar'minta, and you, too."

Minty Lou thought that was a fine story, and as usual she had all sorts of questions to ask. Momma had one, too. She said, "Did you ever think that if Allie had stuck to going off with Harriet Tubman, you might have had some education, Ma?"

"Now I never did think of that. Too busy, I guess. Nor I didn't think neither how I might've been buried in that swamp and never had no education, nor even had my big Lou."

Lou rolled up a pair of socks into a ball and

set them aside. "I'd've run off, Ma, that I would. You'd better believe me."

"Come to think of it," Grandma Minty agreed, "you done run off, you and Jim. You left your kinfolk to home, and you ain't got no real neighbors. Wouldn't so much as've helped out Josepheen if I hadn't made you."

"I'll show you, Ma. I'll take you to the hospital tomorrow."

"Oh, you got that fancy job, but that ain't everything. There's Jim, now, over to Bethl'em Steel. Does he like that?"

Poppa said he did so like it. Leastways he liked the fellers, and he was used to the noise and the dirt and the heat. Just as soon as he could read and write good, he was a-going to get himself a janitor job. Baltimore was all right.

"Grandma Minty, Grandma Minty!" demanded Minty Lou, hopping up and down with impatience. "I asked you, will you sing 'I Got Shoes'?"

Grandma Minty laughed and said that Minty Lou was like her ma, got to have what she wanted. She sung the song, and Poppa joined in it. He said he sure did like that old tune, and there was another that his own pop used to sing afore he run off, and that was "Let the Church Roll On." They all sang that, and Grandma Minty showed them how to make up all kinds of new verses to put in it. Even Momma joined in until they started to giggle, when she said it was bedtime.

The Hospital

MINTY LOU just loved the hospital, where her momma said the kitchen help quit work to spoil her. She did not simply like it because of the tasty bits they popped into her mouth, or even because of all the new questions she got answered. It was the hospital itself. She took a long sniff at the clean, sharp smell of disinfectant as she pointed out a real nurse to Grandma Minty, looking fresh as a painted doll in her blue uniform, black stockings, and starched cap pinned exactly straight on her smooth head.

"Don't point!" reminded Momma. "It isn't good manners."

The nurse took no notice, but walked past about her own business, looking as though she owned the hospital, which Minty Lou rather supposed she did.

"I like that other one better," remarked Grandma Minty.

"Oh, *Gran-ma!* That isn't even a real nurse. That's only a . . . only a . . ."

"Probationer," Momma supplied.

"See how her cap's smaller," cried Minty Lou, eager to instruct. "She dresses different, just to show that she isn't as good as a nurse."

"She was good enough to help that poor man," insisted Grandma Minty. "Where's all the other sick folk?"

Momma explained that they would see the sick folk later. She had brought Grandma Minty in by the front entrance, which she did not often use, just to show her what a huge place the hospital was. The main kitchens and Momma's own office were over thisaway and then downstairs. She led them down to a long corridor, tiled on the sides and on the floor, with doors opening into it. From the far end they could hear dishes clatter. Momma said that everyone in the hospital ate early and that it was nearly time to serve lunch. From the smell, it was stew.

One of the kitchen help came out of a door carrying a cup of coffee. She stopped for an instant to call over her shoulder, "She's back, girls; and you'd better get stepping. It's our Lou."

Six or seven other helpers crowded out, exclaiming that they knowed how Lou wouldn't never stay away a whole week. Was this her ma? What'd ya know? How come they hadn't seen Minty Lou since they couldn't think when? Wouldn't hardly have known her, seeing how big she was growing!

Everybody was smiling and laughing, Momma with the rest; but she said it sure was time for her to come back to work if the girls was off having coffee while there was lunch to be sent up. Didn't they know that head nurse up there on the top floor would skin her alive if lunch was one minute late?

That seemed to be a good joke, but just as they were giggling over it, a man in a cook's cap put his head out of one of the doors lower down to say, "Come on back, girls! What you-all socializing about when there's lunch to be got ready?" His face lit up as he exclaimed, "Why, it's never our Lou! Just as large as life and a bit over! See you, Lou!" He vanished, and the girls dashed after him. Other people popped busy heads out to say briefly, "Hullo, Lou!"

"We'd better get into my office, quick," protested Lou, laughing, "before Edna, that I'm training up to help me, tells me I'm worse than the girls for stopping work." She led the way down a small side passage to a tiny office, crowded by a couple of old desks covered with papers sorted out into neat piles. It was a barren little place with a brown linoleum floor and a window looking onto a gloomy airshaft, calculated to admit the minimum of light and ventilation. Grandma Minty gazed around it unimpressed.

"You're better off to home," she pointed out.

"Besides, you got nothing to do in here but sit looking at papers."

Momma was putting on a fresh white uniform in which her bulk looked jauntier than ever. She rummaged in the top drawer of her desk for a round white button with a big red *S*. "What's that?" asked Minty Lou, who had never seen it.

That badge went with the job which Momma was doing. Every day the nurses sent down orders about what the sick people ought to eat. Today, for instance, there'd be the ordinary lunch and then four or five other kinds for folk that couldn't manage regular food. All these lunches were put into containers and hauled up a shaft to the nurses upstairs. It was important to send the right amount to each floor, depending on what the orders were that came to the kitchens. Momma got the orders and told the cooks how much of each lunch to prepare and where to send it. She tasted the food to make sure it was good, and she inspected the kitchens. She had a good many kitchens besides the big one to cover. There were separate ones for the nurses' dining room, for the doctors', and for a couple of hospital wings a good way off.

The badge was a new idea because when anything went wrong about the food upstairs, Momma had to go talk it over. Upstairs, they weren't used to meeting colored people in the sort of job Momma had been given. Those nurses were just plain rude until the hospital had given her this

badge with *S* for supervisor. It seemed to make
them understand she wasn't just help from the
kitchen.

Minty Lou stared at the badge, awed. It stood out proudly on the white expanse of Momma's uniform, showing clearly that she was better than anybody else. Lou smiled at her expression and produced an extra badge from the drawer. "Would you like to wear one?" She fastened it onto the white pinafore, and Minty Lou hugged her.

Edna came in to go to her desk, looking as though she was in a hurry. Edna wore the red *S* too; but it seemed less important because she was a little person, not like Momma. She said that everything was all right, thank you, except that the top floor was griping as usual. It stood to reason their food got cold; it had farther to go.

"Take it easy, Edna, then. I'll be back Monday."

Edna nodded, adding in a tight little voice, "That Bill's been drinking again."

"Oh-oh!" Lou shook her head. "We warned him, didn't we? Can you handle him, Edna?"

"I . . . guess so."

"You don't need to report him yourself. I'll do it Monday. He's not acting ugly, is he, Edna?"

Edna shook her head. "It's all right, thanks. I can manage." She whisked away, plainly wanting no interference. Lou gazed after her doubtfully.

"Bill's been drinking in bouts ever since his wife left him," she explained to Grandma Minty. "I warned him he'd better not come lit up to work, but he won't listen."

"Poor man," nodded Grandma Minty. "He's lonely, I guess."

"Bill used to be a good cook, but the girls is scared of him half the time now. They won't keep him on."

"Poor man!" repeated Grandma Minty in a soft, reproachful tone.

Lou spread her hands. "Look, Ma, I just run a kitchen where sick people has to be fed. I don't do the hiring. There's plenty of cooks."

Grandma Minty said nothing to that, and after a moment Momma said they'd better go up to a ward and see the sick people now that she'd got her uniform on. It wasn't quite lunchtime, and some of the nicer nurses thought it cheered folks up to see a few new faces outside of visiting hours. She took them upstairs and into a long room with a lot of beds all quite close together. There was a nurse with jolly red cheeks in an office just by the doorway who popped out to say, "Hallo, Lou! You back from your vacation?"

"Just visiting, ma'am."

The nurse said they could go in because she did not expect anyone would be sleeping so soon before lunch. They did go in, and Grandma soon got talking to an old lady that had slipped and broken her leg getting onto a streetcar. She had a grandson called Mike, which was the name of Grandma's youngest boy, so that they got along fine. The old lady said it was awful quiet in the hospital. People didn't seem to talk much, and there wan't nothing to do all day. She felt right low sometimes because she was used to a bustle.

Grandma said she liked to sing when she felt low; and the old lady said she didn't have no breath for singing no more, but she sure loved a tune. Grandma Minty sang her a song very quietly

so as not to wake anyone who might be sleeping,
while the old lady beat time with one hand and
hummed along. One or two people that were lying
close by turned over to listen; and the red-cheeked
nurse came down to say that the ones farther off
were asking if Grandma Minty wouldn't sing to
them all. "They mostly can't read," the nurse said,
"so there's nothing for them to do but remember
they're sick."

Grandma Minty sang, "O What a Beautiful
City" and "Ride on, King Jesus" because they
were happy tunes which were good for sick people.
It was wonderful how some did smile and sit up
a little, looking quite perky. Everyone asked for
another song, but just then there was a rumble
from the shaft where they were hauling lunch
upstairs. The nurse said maybe some other day.
Grandma Minty waved her hand to the old lady,
and nearly everyone waved back. The nurse said
they'd all eat bigger lunches because of having
been cheered up.

As they walked away, Grandma Minty said
she sure did like the hospital, and she wished that
she could come every day to sing to those poor
people.

Momma laughed and told her that not all the
nurses were as nice as this one, and every one of
them liked to have things the way they'd been
planned. "I never did see no one upset folks'
plans like you do."

Grandma Minty started to argue that, but
Momma said in any case it was time to eat lunch.
The kitchen people had theirs right after they
got the food upstairs, so as to get it when it was
good and hot. She wanted Grandma to see what
a big kitchen was like with its huge pots for stew
and spaghetti, its big baking ovens, and all the
great ladles and bowls and everything.

"Can I have red Jell-O? Can I have red Jell-O?"
demanded Minty Lou.

Momma said maybe, but while they were here
in the east wing, they might as well just go past
the east kitchen . . . in case Edna . . . well, she
wanted to look in because of Bill.

They descended to another corridor, rather like
the first one except that the floor was plain cement
and the walls cream. There was the same smell of
onions, only stronger; but everything seemed quiet,
as though the cooking was going on by itself without people to watch it.

"That's funny!" said Momma anxiously.
"Where's everyone got to?" She pushed past the
other two and set off briskly down the corridor,
so that they had to trot to keep up.

This kitchen had double swing doors which had
been fastened open to wheel the trays of food out
to the lift shaft. Momma stopped dead in the en-
tranceway, while Grandma and Minty Lou peered
around her. This kitchen was not as big as the
main one, and there were only some eight or nine

work people in it. All of them were standing perfectly still except one, who was behind a counter
over near the far wall, chopping onions.

He was not a very tall man, but he looked swollen. His cook's cap was pushed back on his head
as though it had grown too small. His cheeks
puffed out as though there were air in them, and
above them his eyes were squinnied up small,
streaming with tears because of the onions. His
hands were fat and dimpled, but they moved rap-
idly, holding his chopper by the handle and rip-
ping an onion out of a sack which lay beside him
to slice it through without so much as peeling off
the yellow skin.

"Whatever do you think you're doing, Bill?"
asked Lou from the doorway.

Eight pairs of frightened eyes moved in her direction, but no one in the kitchen said anything
except Bill himself, who replied briefly, "Chopping onions!" With a contemptuous flick, he shoved
the pieces down the counter to join a large pile in
front of Edna, whom he had somehow managed to
wedge between the wall and his person. Tears were
rolling down Edna's cheeks because of the onions,
and she shut her eyes. Bill chuckled ferociously as
he grabbed with his free hand for another onion.

Lou took a couple of steps into the kitchen.
"That's got beyond a joke, Bill, now. Leave Edna
alone."

Bill's right hand picked up a rolling pin which

lay beside him, while his left hand paused with the chopper raised above the onion. "*You* stop! You stop right there, big Lou, and don't come no nearer. I'd just as soon smash you . . . or her." He flourished the rolling pin at Edna. "Going about behind my back to get me fired! Sneaking up behind so that I'll lose my head and do something silly! You're all the same," he said, glaring around the kitchen. "All out to get me, every one of you. I'll show you!" He lowered his chopper, thudding down on the board with rhythmical strokes. Edna opened her streaming eyes and sent a glance at Lou, while she shrank a little closer to the wall.

"Now, Bill, you know you can't act thisaway," said Lou reasonably. "A joke's a joke, but this one's gone far enough. You just put that rolling pin down now, Bill, and leave Edna alone." She began to walk forward the length of the kitchen with un-hurried steps, while Bill, the rolling pin still held high, watched her out of reddened eyes. He growled what might have been a warning at her, but nobody, even in the silence of the kitchen, could make out the words.

Lou came right up against the counter on one side, while Bill backed away about a foot on the other. She held out her hand. "Hadn't you better give me that, Bill?" she said, her eyes on the roll-ing pin.

Edna gave a little squeal and tried to jump him. He knocked her impatiently back against the wall

with his free hand and, almost in the same movement, sent the rolling pin flying through the air at
Lou. "You asked for it!" he yelled.

Lou was too close to dodge, but she threw up
her hand a little, and it crashed against her arm
with a horrible thud and clattered to the floor. The
kitchen seemed to resound with the noise of it and
the horrified gasps that followed. Bill put his hands
up to his sore eyes. "She asked for it, didn't she?
You heard her! Wouldn't leave me do my job.
Come around where she wasn't wanted, like always, didn't she? Couldn't take a joke . . . just a
joke!" He gave a choked howl, meant for laughter,
which ended in sobbing.

Lou slipped around the counter to put her good
arm around his shoulders. "Here, Molly, fetch
over that stool for Bill to set on. Tom, get the doctor from the desk upstairs and look slippy! Get me
a glass of water for Bill." She patted his shoulder.
"There, that's better!"

Pretty soon the doctor came in running, and he
gave Bill something that looked nasty to drink.
Two men in white uniforms appeared and helped
him away. The doctor mixed a drink for Edna,
too; and he sent her off to have a lay-down because
she was crying in great sobs and trembling all over.
Lou held her arm against her chest and said it
wasn't much, only not to touch it, please. It'd be
all right after a while, but she looked gray.

The doctor said that maybe something was broken; but he dared say it wasn't too bad, for all it hurt. She'd have to go easy on it, though, for a little while. He took her away to have a better look, but he told Grandma not to worry.

Everyone in the kitchen poured out cups of coffee and said how their hearts had almost stopped beating and how Bill had scared the life out of them for the last week. Then they all had some stew, with Jello-O and a dab of real whipped cream for Minty Lou. They all said how brave her momma was and how they dassn't so much as move a step when she walked right up that room. Minty Lou did not say as much as usual because she had been frightened. She listened while everyone told Grandma what a wonderful person her momma was and how all the kitchen help adored her.

Momma came back after a while with her arm all bandaged and inside a great sling. She said there was a little bone broken, but nothing too bad and that the doctor had fixed it up real nice so that it felt better. Poor Bill had a sort of breakdown, and the doctors had taken charge of him. Grandma thought they had better go home so that Momma could take it easy.

"Why, I forgot to put back your badge," said Momma two hours later when they were home and she was taking it easy trying to shell peas with one hand. "You'd better let me have it."

Minty Lou put her own hand over the white button with the red *S* on it. "Can't I get to keep it?" she asked, her face falling.

Momma considered. "Well, I guess there's plenty more, and no one wouldn't stop to mind. So if you want it . . ."

Minty Lou went to sleep that night with the red *S* under her pillow. "When I grow up," she whispered to Grandma as they said good night, "I'm going to have a white uniform and wear my button. Only I can be a real nurse, too, Momma says . . ."

Grandma kissed her and said she expected all the best nurses in the hospital got to wear buttons.

Mr. Prince's Luck

GRANDMA MINTY went home for the corn and
tomato picking, and Momma was sorry to see her
go. She said she didn't like her working like a
field hand, stooping over all the day long in the
hot sun. She said she didn't like her living in that
shack either, drawing her water out of the well in
a bucket. Grandma said she was used to it, but
Momma said them things grew worse when you
got older; and she sure did hate to think of her
and Grandpa living that way. But there weren't
never enough work for folks in Cambridge, not
even for them that did a good job, like Grandpa.
She kissed Grandma and cried over her a bit; and
Minty Lou felt sorry for her, too. It must be terrible to live that way, never knowing whether the
salt pork and the barrel of flour and the wood
that Grandpa chopped would last the winter, when
there wasn't money coming in.

Lou went back to the hospital in spite of her
arm, and Minty Lou went back to play school

while she was at work. Play school was old Mrs.
Williams's front parlor, where the kids played
games or sat around on wet days, while on good
days they went two blocks down and over two to
the park, where they could play catch and tag
and things like that. Play school was rather boring
because there was not much to do. Minty Lou
liked real school better, and come September she
went into the second grade with a new teacher.

Mr. Prince and Josepheen were still upstairs.
Jim and Lou went off Saturday nights to dance at
the Pavilion, where Mr. Prince had introduced
them to the Merry Band. Lou had made herself a
blue dress and bought Jim a blue tie to match with
a pink bird on it, standing right out as though you
could pick it off. Minty Lou just loved that bird.
She still did not like Mr. Prince because he had
found out how she hid when she heard he was
coming. He had started to sneak up on her and
jump out, crying, "Boo!"

When Jim and Lou were all dressed up, they
showed off to Minty Lou before they went out. She
admired them very much, her momma so big and
shiny, and her poppa so neat in his snappy pinstripe that he got at the pawnshop and everyone
said was a good buy. Josepheen, who never went
out because of the baby, stayed home with Minty
Lou. Momma always left them something special
for their supper, maybe a piece of cake or a bit of
candy.

Minty Lou rather liked her evenings with Josepheen. She was pretty dull and couldn't answer questions; but she liked to listen, and she always said, "Oh, my!" Minty Lou chattered along about school or about the little girl down at the shop on the corner who had a doll made out of a black stocking she called Molly, and who called Minty Lou Molly whenever she saw her. Sometimes she made stories up; but even when they were a bit unlikely, Josepheen never caught her out as Lou would have done. She just opened her eyes a little wider as she said, "Oh, my!" She never minded if Minty Lou talked about bad luck signs or spoke sloppy, like she did around other kids. She even agreed to learn to read, which school never managed to teach her; but lessons always ended with Minty Lou reading the book and Josepheen saying, "Oh, my!"

The nicest thing about Josepheen was that she disliked Mr. Prince as much as Minty Lou did. She was scared of him, and she said that Arthureen always yelled when he went by. Besides, he complained about the smells in the bathroom, as if babies didn't all smell. Josepheen said quite a lot about Mr. Prince besides, "Oh, my!" She even giggled when Minty Lou made up stories about terrible things that happened to him.

An evening with Josepheen was quite good fun, so that Minty Lou went happily to bed in the dark house while Mr. Prince was working at the Pa-

vilion and Lou and Jim were dancing, "See Me
Dance the Polka!" under the lights, up and down
and around and back again, bouncing higher than
anybody else in the big room. Sometimes they
even danced right out of the window, Momma
said, and went up and down the big gallery that
was built out over the water, with the stars shining bright and the air cool.

Minty Lou felt so safe with Josepheen that she
never stayed awake until her momma came home.
Sunday mornings they all got up late, which made
a scramble to get Minty Lou to Sunday school on
time. When somebody came knocking at the street
door one Sunday early when the light was still
gray in the sky, Minty Lou did not exactly know
what to do. Her room was right over the front,
so naturally she heard it; but Momma and Pop
never stirred. Somebody was shouting, "Let me
in!" loud enough to wake all the neighbors. She
took a peep out of the window, wondering if Mr.
Prince had forgotten his key; but it wasn't a man's
voice at all. She could not see much because it
was one of those late fall days when mornings are
misty.

She tiptoed across the hall to Momma's room,
but the door was not closed and there was nobody
in it. The moment she put her head inside, she
could feel that it was empty. Besides, she could
dimly see in the dark that the white spread had
not been taken off.

Something clutched at Minty Lou like falling from the top of a big building, which she did now and then in a dream. Whenever she dreamed that, she woke screaming; and she screamed now. She yelled, "Josepheen!" at the top of her voice and dashed upstairs, stumbling over a step and bumping her knee in her hurry.

Josepheen was sitting up in bed listening to the noise. Minty Lou leaped over the box where Arthureen slept and jumped onto the bed. She flung her arms around Josepheen's neck and said, "They didn't come home!"

"Who didn't come home?" asked Josepheen in her silly way. But she patted Minty Lou; and presently she said in a frightened voice, "It's nearly morning." Minty Lou buried her face on Josepheen's shoulder and shuddered. Presently Josepheen tried again.

"That's them at the door," she said in a weary tone as though she were used to this sort of thing. "They're just drunk, honey."

Minty Lou shook her head against Josepheen's neck.

The noise downstairs did not stop . . . bang, bang, and then a shout, "Let me in!", and then another shout for Josepheen.

Josepheen unclasped Minty Lou and went to the window, putting her head out to yell, "There's nobody to-home."

"You come down and let me in, Josepheen! I'm

that poor dear child's Grandma, that's left all
alone without nobody else to care for her. I come
as soon as . . . as soon as . . ." Grandma broke
down and cried in the open street, and Minty Lou
heard her. The bottom dropped once and for all
out of Minty Lou's world.

Grandma cried a lot more over Minty Lou until
her hair felt wet, but Minty Lou did not cry herself. She listened to Grandma tell how Momma
and Poppa had danced out onto the gallery at the
Pavilion, going one–two–three–bounce, one–two–
three–bounce, leading the parade like they always
did. Then that little old gallery, that was a rotten
thing like the whole Pavilion, just naturally crum-
bled and fell down with the weight of the people
swinging on it. Mr. Prince, who was passing the
window with a tray of drinks, saw Momma and
Poppa go off into the water with a screaming
mass of people on top. When the police officers
came, he told them they'd best go to Grandma and
leave her to break the news to Minty Lou. That
poor kid, he said, all alone in the house next morning! Then he said he sure was a lucky man because
he had stepped out on that gallery himself a minute before.

Minty Lou listened without saying anything or
really feeling either. She did not move because she
did not want to come to life and have to think, or
say, or do. After a time, Grandma wiped her own
eyes and said Minty Lou should dress and eat some

breakfast. She went down to the kitchen where Josepheen was lighting the stove, and she came back
in a little while with a glass of milk. Minty Lou
was still sitting on the edge of the bed in her nightgown, shivering with cold.

Grandma spoke quite sharply, putting the glass
into Minty Lou's hand, and telling her to drink it.
She did raise it to her lips, but her throat closed
up so that she could not swallow. She started to
choke.

Grandma took the milk away and told Josepheen, who was coming up the stairs, that the
child was acting crazy — didn't seem to mind that
her parents were dead, never shed so much as a
tear, but wouldn't do nothing, not even look up
and speak to her own grandma.

Josepheen didn't answer that, but she came in
quietly, lifted Minty Lou off her bed, and stood
her on the floor. She found clothes and started to
dress her, buttoning her into her drawers and her
petticoat, slipping on her garters, and lifting one
foot at a time to put on her stockings, as though
she knew without being told that Minty Lou didn't
want to move. She shook her head over the dress
that Momma had put out for Sunday, and she
found a dark blue one instead on the hooks behind
the curtain in one corner. The button with the
red *S* was lying on the bureau. Minty Lou wore it
on her pinafore on Sundays because Momma said
it was not right for school. Josepheen looked at it

for a minute, and then she fastened it on. She took
Minty Lou by one hand to lead her down into the
kitchen, and it seemed all right to go along as long
as one did not move alone.

Grandma was in the kitchen, bringing food out
of the icebox to pack into an orange crate she'd
found on the porch. She said, "No use letting good
things go to waste. Rent's paid till the end of the
month, if I know Lou. That gives you and Mr.
Prince time to look around."

Josepheen's mouth opened, and her eyes popped
with dismay. She hadn't thought that she'd have
to find somewhere to live, nor yet that she was going to be left alone in the house with Mr. Prince.
She said timidly, "Is he coming back?"

"Just as soon as he can," Grandma said, encour-
aging her. "He was . . ." She looked at Minty
Lou and changed her mind about what she was
going to say. "He was helping, you know."

Minty Lou came to life inside a little. She
wanted to get out of the house before Mr. Prince
came back. It was his fault that . . . well, the Pavilion was his fault. She actually moved up to the
kitchen table where Grandma was packing.

"I'll put the kid up some clothes," Josepheen
said, "just for tonight." She found a paper bag
and tied it around with string before she put it
into Minty Lou's hand. Grandma was looking at
the orange crate which still had room at the top.
Making up her mind, she darted into the dining

room and brought out Momma's cut-glass bowl
with the wax fruit in it. "Ain't nobody else got no
use for it," she said to Josepheen in an angry voice.

A few hours after that, Minty Lou sat on one
side of Grandma's kitchen table, while the three
kids sat on the other side. They whispered among
themselves, but they did not seem to know what to
say to Minty Lou. Presently Gordie bounced up
from his chair. "I guess there's a job I got to do
outside."

Bert giggled. "I guess I got a job as much as
you."

Tom got up without saying anything and followed them out.

Minty Lou sat alone. Grandma had gone off,
saying that there was things to be done and that
the kids should look after that poor child. They
did stick around for a while, but the kitchen was
quieter without them.

Grandma was never a one for asking people
over, so that Minty Lou had not often been into
her kitchen, which was a basement room with little
windows looking out onto people's feet as they
went by on the sidewalk. It was gloomy and small,
crowded with the coal stove, a pile of boxes, a narrow cupboard, and a small cold-water sink without a drainboard. The middle of the room was
taken up by a table, on which a few dishes were
piled as though there were nowhere else to put

them. Minty Lou wished she weren't there. It was
something to think of.

Grandma came back hot and angry, her breath
going in and out as though she had been hurrying.
She'd come for Minty Lou, who'd got to pull herself together like a big girl. She'd got to look at
her pa and ma in the morgue and sign a paper, or
they wouldn't be let to have a funeral. "I ain't no
kin to your ma," said Grandma, wiping her face
with a trembling hand. "Nor I can't write my
name to nothing neither and so I told him. Did
you hear what I said?"

Minty Lou still would not talk, but she nodded
her head.

"Cat got your tongue," demanded Grandma
sharply, too upset for more patience. "You got
nothing to do but say to the feller in charge, 'This
is my ma and pa.' Then you puts your name to a
paper and that's all." She shook a quivering finger
at Minty Lou. "See here, you didn't do no crying
when there was time for it. There ain't no time for
it now. You understand?"

Minty Lou nodded again.

The morgue was a dirty brick building with a
hall where other people were standing around.
There was a man at a desk with a beefy face who
said to Grandma, "Here, you can't take in that
kid!"

"If you want your paper writ," retorted Grandma, trembling again, "she's got to go see. What's

more, that ma of hers weren't no kin of mine. Her
and her dancing!"

The beefy man looked at Minty Lou for a minute, and he asked, "Don't she *mind?*" as though
he was wondering if black folk did not feel like
other people. Grandma pinched her arm, and she
shook her head.

"I give up!" the beefy man said. "I guess I've
seen everything!" He called down the passage behind him, "Pass that kid in!"

There was a pale, stringy man inside in an over-
all. He looked surprised, too; but he reckoned he
had to get his paper signed. "It's my job," he said
defensively to Grandma, "just doing what I'm
paid for."

Grandma took Minty Lou by the arm and led
her across to where people were lying on a sort of
table covered by a sheet. She did what she was
told and looked as he pulled sheets back. She
couldn't seem to recognize the faces, only the blue
dress that was not shiny anymore, and the pink
bird on the blue tie. She spoke up quickly, shutting
her eyes. "That's my momma. That's my poppa."
They led her over to a book, and she wrote slowly
in her big round hand, "Araminta Louisa Payson."
She wrote it twice, once for each.

They walked out again past the desk, where the
beefy man leaned forward to see if she had been
crying. He threw out his hands and shrugged his
shoulders. Then he made out some writing and

gave it to Grandma, telling her to hand it to the funeral parlor. They walked out down the block, and Minty Lou threw up on the pavement. Then she started to cry because of the taste in her mouth.

Grandma

GRANDMA COOKED MEAT on Saturdays, so that
there was usually cold pork with bread for the
rest of the week. On that first Sunday there was
fried liver out of Momma's icebox, but Minty
Lou could not eat any. For supper there were
boiled beans which Grandma had soaking since
breakfast. Arlene and Joe were home by then, and
there was no spare chair. Grandma fixed up the
orange crate for Minty Lou to sit on while she ate
one or two beans. Luckily there was Momma's
milk, and Minty Lou had some of that. Gordie
wanted a share; but Grandma told him, quite
sharply too, to let the poor kid alone. Arlene said
that Gordie was spoiled rotten, and how was he
going to like not being the youngest?

Grandma tried to pet Minty Lou a little, but she
could not make any impression. Presently she
asked if it wouldn't feel good to go to bed. Minty
Lou nodded; and then because Grandma was being kind she made an effort and said, "Yes."

Grandma took her upstairs and fixed a bed for her out of two quilts on the floor between her own bed and the bureau. She kissed her and said not to let the boys disturb her when they came bumbling in. Then she left her alone.

Next day, Grandma made her get up first and creep down in her nightgown, past the dining room and parlor on the ground floor into the kitchen, where she huddled in one of her quilts near the cold stove till Grandma came down and blew up the fire. Presently the kids had their clothes on and came down to wash. Grandma gave Minty Lou a little basin of water that wasn't too warm and told her to take it upstairs and wash and dress. Be sure not to spill it, and bring it downstairs to empty. The toilet was outside the back door and there was only the kitchen sink inside the house.

After breakfast, which was cold beans fried up and a little molasses, with milk for Minty Lou, they went to school. The kids showed her the way, and Gordie took her into the second grade to explain to the teacher how she had come to live with her grandma. Minty Lou did not try to make friends, either that day or later. She was big for her age, and she soon got the other kids in the class to leave her alone. She did her sums right and said, "Yes, ma'am," when she was spoken to. School was not too bad.

They went home to lunch — it was only a block.

Before she left for work, Grandma had fixed four
plates with cold pork, bread, and pickle. She kept
the icebox locked because it was on the back porch.
Minty Lou had had a hard time eating those beans
for breakfast, and there was no one around to make
her eat lunch. It was easier to let the kids gobble
her share, but in the afternoon she felt dizzy.

Grandma got off early from work and went to
see about the insurance. She told Arlene all about
it in the kitchen while the kids were out. Minty
Lou, who had crept into the parlor upstairs, sat
and listened. "There's enough for the funeral and
a nice bit over," Grandma said. "I'll say that for
Lou, she did fix them things up. Jim, now he was
easygoing."

Arlene said something which was drowned in
the splashing of the tap as she filled the kettle.

"Ar'minta Hayes?" said Grandma sharply.
"Why for would she get any? She don't so much
as know they're dead, much less how to bury them
decent. Nor she can't take the kid. Sam'l never
has no work but the gravedigging, or ditching and
cutting wood when he can get it. They mostly
starves in winter, and they ain't got no room. I'm
her grandma, ain't I? The man at the insurance
didn't ask no questions, so long as I told him the
kid can write her own name to the paper."

"She's gone off somewhere," Arlene remarked.
"Funny kid, that!"

"Put on them greens to boil," Grandma replied. "She'll be back when she's hungry."

Minty Lou had dropped out of sight of her old neighbors, who did not come to the funeral, near Grandma's across town. They did not, for one thing, know when it was; and they could not take time out of work. They shook heads over the accident and said it was terrible for that poor kid, who was such a bright little thing. The teacher at Sunday school asked about her from the other kids, who said she had gone to her grandma's. The teacher in the second grade did the same. There were one or two forms filled out that Minty Lou never heard of; but it turned out she was going to school all right, and that was that. The only person that took the trouble to see what had happened to her arrived in the mid-afternoon before Grandma got out of work. The kids were home, and Minty Lou was sitting by herself in the parlor. She saw him coming out of the window and had time to escape to the bedroom, where she perched on the edge of Grandma's bed, her heart in her mouth.

Mr. Prince rapped at the door, and Gordie opened to him, after grumbling because Tom and Bert had made him do it. Mr. Prince asked for Minty Lou; and Gordie, who did not know or care where she was, said, "She's out."

Mr. Prince would not go away, so that Gordie

had to think of something. He said she was playing with some other kids down the block. Mr.
Prince said he was glad she was making friends,
and was she happy? Gordie told him that she was
quite all right. Mr. Prince asked if the other
grandma — he sure had liked that Mrs. Hayes —
came up to the funeral. Gordie did not like to say
no flat out, so he said she had been sick.

Mr. Prince said that somehow he hadn't been
able to get that poor kid out of his mind, but he
felt better now. He fumbled in his pocket and took
out a whole ten dollar bill. He looked at Gordie
and put it back again, saying that he wanted
Minty Lou's folks just to know that if she needed
anything, he'd be glad to help out as much as he
could. He'd go down the block and see if he saw
her around.

Gordie went back downstairs, while Minty Lou
crept into the parlor to listen. Bert and Gordie
were arguing that it made no sense to tell Ma because they'd never get a smell of Mr. Prince's
money. Best wait and see what they could pick up
themselves. Minty Lou was afraid that Tom would
tell, but he forgot to. She never did see Mr. Prince
again. Perhaps he felt so much better that he
stopped worrying about her, or perhaps Gordie
and Bert did get some money out of him. She never
knew.

Gordie had never liked Minty Lou because she
got attention which he was used to having for him-

self. Right from the beginning when she came to stay with them, he started to tease her. She did not seem to notice at first; but his ma, who had always let him do what he liked, cuffed him for it. It made him more eager than ever to pay Minty Lou back.

Tom and Bert did not want to tease her, but to use her for after-school errands, which Grandma was always giving to them instead of to Gordie. For instance, Grandma could never get far enough ahead to buy her coal by the load, or even by the sack. She doled out a quarter for a bag of coal, which lasted a day in the winter, and in the summer for about half of the week. She bought a block of ice on Saturdays, which the iceman put into the box on the porch. After it melted, they had to do without, going down to the grocery just before meals for perishable goods.

Needing Minty Lou for this kind of errand, Tom and Bert soon discovered that she never went out after school. She crept into the living room, which they never entered from one week's end to the other. There she sat, cool as you please, on one of Grandma's stuffed chairs, resting her school-book on the round, lace-covered table, almost touching the cut-glass bowl with the fruit that had been her mother's. Tom and Bert were so astonished at her nerve that they left her alone.

The moment Gordie heard where she was, he bounced upstairs and started to tease her about being too high and mighty to sit in the kitchen. Minty Lou had not said much these days because she did not want to, but it never occurred to her to hold back if she did. She had always said just what she pleased and had been praised for it. When Gordie went on and on, Minty Lou retorted with exactly what she thought. "I don't want to

live here. This house is dirty, and the toilet stinks.
Besides, the pork smelled that we had for lunch."
This was true, and Gordie hadn't eaten it either.

Gordie was furious. He said, "I suppose this
room isn't good enough for you either."

Minty Lou said, "It's dark and ugly, and the
things are all banged up. The dining room's worse.
I wish I was home." She put her head down on
the lace tablecloth and cried. Gordie pinched her,
but she took no notice. Even he did not dare start
a fight in this room, so he went away and waited
to tell his ma.

Any of the neighbors who had been questioned
about Grandma would have said she was not a bad
sort, though a little rough. The roughness was due
to the hard time she'd had with a no-good husband, who'd left her in the end with all those kids.
She'd done all right, moving to the city and getting steady work. Arlene, that might have gone
to the bad, was respectably married. Come next
birthday, Tom could quit school. The neighbors
felt sorry for Grandma for having Minty Lou left
on her hands just at the moment when some of the
other kids were growing up. It never occurred to
them to worry about Minty Lou.

Grandma was outraged by the story that Gordie
told her, the more so because her mouth had
watered over Lou's furniture. She had refrained
from taking it just because she needed money with
another mouth to feed. This thought reminded her

that the funeral parlor was getting too much of the insurance money that she had expected to have with Minty Lou. One way and another, her temper boiled over. She cuffed Minty Lou for sitting upstairs and threatened to whip her for dirtying up the good rooms and wearing the furniture. What was more, she yelled, Minty Lou was a spoiled brat, spoiled rotten by her mother. She never had liked Lou, and this kid was her image. "Setting up there in my good rooms like a fine lady! You can make yourself some use for once and dust the both of them, and be sure you do it good, or I'll get enough notion to take a strap to you."

Minty Lou had been whipped by her momma for being naughty, but she never had been yelled at, cuffed and shaken, or called names. She was scared deep down inside, but she was also resentful. All the time she was dusting with extra care, she kept on thinking that it was not really wrong to sit in the parlor and that Grandma ought not to have said what she did about Momma. She did a good job with the dusting; only it was no fun, as it always used to be when she and Momma had played a game of catching each other out neglecting corners.

Grandma was not the sort that forgot things once they had been said or done. It was true that she always used to spoil Minty Lou, but it was one thing to admire her starched pinafores or her pert questions when her own mother had the washing

and ironing to do. Though envious, Grandma had
been proud of the way that Jim and Lou lived, as
well as of a grandchild that was a little doll and
a credit to her. But once she had lost her temper
with the child, she could see that the brat was
spoiled rotten. Once she had listened to Minty
Lou's frank opinion, as told by Gordie, of her
household, she could not forgive her. Nor was the
child cute anymore. Grandma could hardly look
at her, sitting hunched up small, without thinking
how the brat was never once grateful to her
grandma, nor kissed her, nor cared at all when
her own parents died.

"I'm not 'Min,' " the brat said sulkily. "I'm
Minty Lou."

It was said to Gordie, not to Grandma, but it
served to boil irritation over. Who did she think
she was, she and her mother with their fancy
names? "Araminta Louisa!" With her pink bows
and party dresses and starched pinafores! She'd
learn right soon that these airs would not do.

"Was that my party dress," demanded Minty
Lou, "hanging up in the pawnship? I saw it today."

"Well, and why not?" screamed Grandma, giving her a hearty cuff. "What were you doing wan-
dering the streets and getting into mischief?"

"I was fetching the coal," Minty Lou muttered,
"for Tom and Bert."

This answer pleased Grandma no better. Tom

and Bert could run their own errands without the help of a great girl sitting idle while other folk worked to earn her keep. Why didn't Min wash the stairs tomorrow if she thought the house was dirty? Grandma made her fetch bucket and scrub brush from the back porch, found her the end of a bar of soap, and showed her how to scrub and how to wipe up with a rag.

"I'll leave some water on the stove that you can dip out when you get back from school. It'll still be warm. If you spill it all over the place, I'll give you a whipping."

Threats of whipping led to whippings in fact. Washing the stairs led to scrubbing the kitchen and even to doing the laundry. Minty Lou had to boil the clothes in a big pan, stirring with a paddle and standing on a chair in order to reach. Then she had to slide it off the fire, dip out boiling water, and pour in enough cold to put her hands in. Next came endless scrubbing of bad spots, squeezing, rinsing in another pan set on the table, and squeezing again. The clothes had to be hung on the back porch and the kitchen mopped up. Minty Lou always spilled a good deal, and on one occasion she poured boiling water over her hand.

"Aren't you a bit hard on Min?" asked Arlene good-naturedly on this occasion. Arlene worked long hours and spent most of her free time with Joe lounging about town. She did little household work, but Grandma knew that in self-defense a

woman has to do what is demanded by her man.
All the same it was not right for Arlene to lecture
as long as she did not lend a hand more often.

"Hard!" Grandma snapped. "Why shouldn't
that brat have it hard? I was doing laundry when
I was five year old, and she's seven. I was hauling
the water in a bucket from the well. And I didn't
have no school to go to and sit idle half the day.
My dad beat me when he got drunk which was
most evenings. She don't know what hard is."

Arlene shrugged. After all, she had it hard, too,
when she was a kid. Still . . . "You ain't that
hard on Gordie," she pointed out.

"Gordie's a man," said Grandma, not bothering to explain to Arlene how it was no use expecting a man to do women's work. Tom and Bert
were too big for her to thrash. Gordie wasn't, but
whatever she did to him, he'd follow the others'
example. Grandma kept her kids in order by
screaming at them and dealing out sundry cuffs,
while actually she let them do pretty much what
they pleased. It worked well enough. When Tom
left school, she'd see to it that he brought some of
his money home. For the present, she let him keep
what he made by delivering papers or groceries to
folks. As a result, he was not anxious to leave home
and pay rent. She knew what she was at.

"The brat's quite handy," she said, summing
up her thoughts. "I got to go to church last Sunday, which I ain't done in I dunno how many

months." She reflected. "There's lots of kids goes
out to work at seven. I wan't but six myself. She's
got her Saturdays, and it'd be a help with her
keep."

"You sure are chintzy, Ma," replied Arlene
with appreciation.

The Big Fight

MINTY LOU was indeed getting handy at rough cleaning and even cooking of a sort. Grandma's own housekeeping was slapdash, but she had worked in white people's houses and knew what was done there. Her method was to show Minty Lou a task just once, and then whip her if it was not done right. Like most of Grandma's ways, it worked pretty well.

It was no use making friends in school by now because Minty Lou never got time to play with them. Grandma did not believe in play for girls, especially if they were a burden on people that had their own kids to bring up. Minty Lou's school clothes, that used to be so fresh and pretty, had become a washed-out gray never starched anymore. Arlene had showed her how to cobble her stockings together, but she dared not run about in the playground lest she fall down. Knee holes were beyond her.

The worst about Grandma was that she never

let up. If Minty Lou worked hard, she got no thanks for it. Her name was not even Min by now, but "Brat," the living image of that Lou that was a bad wife to Jim, and had killed him in the end with her flighty ways.

Minty Lou did not say anything to this sort of abuse. She had even learned to hold her tongue when Gordie teased her. She wore Momma's button with the big red *S* under her dress because Gordie snatched at it. It was the only thing she had besides her clothes, and there was nowhere to keep it. But it did not mean much anymore, now that Momma was gone.

She went about her chores after school; and if there was any time over, she fetched and carried for the boys, who took their tone from Grandma. But though she seemed quite cowed, inside she was learning to hate.

She started off, of course, by hating Grandma. She would sit at the table hating the way Grandma tore at her food. She would listen to Grandma's voice, hating the screeching tone without hearing what was said. She would hate her snoring or the creak when she turned over in bed, deliberately lying awake in her two quilts on the floor to hate harder.

The poison of hate in a house is always felt. Grandma cuffed Minty Lou for staring at her. She looked at the floor instead, hating Grandma's shoes and the flat way she put her foot down.

Grandma yelled at her for a sullen little brat spoiled by a no-good mother. Minty Lou did not answer back, but hate consumed her.

She did not hate Gordie at first, even though he jeered at her and pinched her and told tales about her to Grandma. Gordie was an equal more or less. She could not like him, but she did not need to waste on him the kind of venom that was her only weapon against Grandma. But when she no longer dared to stare at Grandma, she looked at Gordie instead. She began to hate the way he blinked his eyes like Grandma and the shape of his head, that was the image of hers. Dislike and hate began to merge. She soon hated Gordie for his own malicious nature. She hated Tom for being a great unfeeling lump; she hated Bert; she hated Arlene for doing no work and not taking her part. She hated them all.

"It's the quiet ones that get me," remarked the second-grade teacher. "There's a girl in my class that doesn't do anything that you can put a finger on. Well, it wouldn't surprise me if that one pulled out a knife one day. Believe me, that kid is bad news."

"What's her name?" asked the third-grade teacher, faintly interested in what was likely to come her way the following year.

"Min Payson. The children know; none of them go near her."

The third-grade teacher groaned. "Not Gordie's

sister! I've got Gordie now, and believe me . . ."

"Give me Gordie!" the second-grade teacher said. "He's a little beast, but he's *normal*."

Minty Lou was hating the second-grade kids and the teacher only in a distant way. She was wrestling with the desire to break out, but not irrationally, as the teacher thought she might. She was trying to nerve herself to fight with Gordie.

Ever since that first week when her throat would not swallow, the kids had been laying claim to Minty Lou's lunch. By getting out of school on time and running home quickly, she managed to eat it once or twice a week. Unluckily for her, the second-grade teacher was one of the fussy ones who liked to have everything put neat before the children went, so that most times one of the kids got home before her. With all the heavy work she was doing after school, she needed that lunch. She had not said anything because she did not suppose it would do any good, but swallowed tears were no help with the housework, while she never got more than her usual share for supper. It was no use appealing to Grandma, who would tell her to settle that with the kids. Besides, she could not bring herself to ask Grandma's help.

Minty Lou watched the boys in the schoolyard fighting with one another and sometimes getting rough. She thought she would like to be rough herself with Gordie, and even with Tom or Bert. The big boys would hurt her a great deal more

that she hurt them; but she had to make them
leave her lunch alone. She was starving, and all
her dresses were too loose.

This was such a big decision that Minty Lou
did not know she had made it until she got home
one day to find the three of them just finishing up.
Something took hold of her and caused her to say
in a loud, angry tone, "I'm hungry. Where's my
lunch?"

Bert and Tom, to do them justice, looked a bit
sheepish. Gordie laughed, rubbing his stomach.
"Wouldn't you just like to know, eh? Perhaps Ma
didn't fix it." He put out his tongue.

"Oh, shut up!" Minty Lou put her legs apart and
her hands on her hips in imitation of the bully of
the second grade. "I got a right to eat, just the
same as you. If any one of you touches my food,
I'll beat on him. I'll hurt him." She really meant
what she said. Her sincerity penetrated even Tom's
thick head. He said slowly,

"Better lay off her, kids. Min's right. It's her
lunch."

Bert nodded, but Gordie jeered, "Don't she
hope she can get it!"

Minty Lou slept badly that night; and in school
she did not pay attention, so that Teacher had to
speak to her twice — a thing which never happened. When lunchtime came, she wanted to hurry
home and get there first; but common sense told
her she had better have things out. She actually

waited until the other classes had gone before she walked home slowly, clenching her hands into fists, her heart in her mouth.

All three of the kids were ahead of her. Tom and Bert were finishing their own plates. Gordie had gobbled his up and started on Minty Lou's.

"That's my lunch," Minty Lou yelled, striking her attitude. "You got no right to eat my lunch!"

"That's so," agreed Tom, too lazy to interfere with a fight. "I told you not to take it, Gordie."

Gordie looked at Tom and then at Minty Lou. Slowly, deliberately he put back what was left on the plate, spat on it and held it out to Minty Lou. "Here, take your lunch!"

"I'm going to fight," screamed Minty Lou, trembling on the edge of action. "I'm going to whup you."

"Come on, Bert," Tom said. "Let the kid teach Gordie a lesson." They went out, not bothering to see fair play, but at least admitting that Minty Lou had reason to fight their brother.

Gordie did not wait to be attacked. He picked up a kitchen chair and rushed at Minty Lou, swinging hard. She dodged around the table and threw a plate at him. It hit the chair and broke. She threw another and connected with Gordie's ear. He gave a howl and came at her again.

She got a blow on the back, stopping to pick up the broom. The chair nearly knocked her down, but she was too excited to care. She turned and whacked at Gordie. He whirled the chair again with all his force, but it hit the wall as she dodged, broke the plaster and went in. He tugged it out, but she caught his arm with the broom, and he dropped it. It was his turn now to run around the table. He pushed one of the other chairs in Minty Lou's way. She stumbled past it, throwing aside the broom which was awkward for close quarters, pinned Gordie into a corner and pummeled his eye. He hit back, cutting her lip, but she did not so much as turn her face away. He butted with his head, forcing her backward while she got in a blow on the ear that was hit by the plate.

Minty Lou tripped over the chair behind her and fell, rolling desperately to get out of the way. But Gordie did not fall on top of her or even kick. He was fumbling in the kitchen table drawer for Grandma's knife which she kept to slice the pork. It was pointed and sharp.

Minty Lou scrambled up a good deal frightened and got the table between herself and the knife. Gordie leaned over it to slash at her hand, which was gripping the table edge. "I'll naturally cut you to pieces!" he yelled.

She had no doubt that he would, but she had to win or starve. Desperate for a weapon, she picked up the kettle. It was a cheap tin one, but half full of water and heavy. Spraying water out of the spout, she swung it at Gordie as he made a wild slash with the knife. Perhaps both of them

were a little scared of what they were doing because the knife only ripped down her sleeve, scor-
ing a long shallow gash in her arm. The kettle,
meanwhile, missed Gordie's face completely except for the underlip of the spout, made of tin
and sharp. It caught Gordie under the nose.

Gordie screamed and clapped his left hand to
his face, blood streaming through his fingers. But

Minty Lou could not have stopped if she tried.
She swung the kettle again with her full strength
and caught him clean on the side of the head.
Gordie made a queer sound and fell, head under
the table. Minty Lou put down the kettle with a
trembling hand and walked out.

Bert and Tom were lingering in the yard,
through which they went by the back gate to

school. They looked a little anxious at the sudden silence in the kitchen and the sight of Minty Lou with blood running down her arm. "Is he dead?" asked Bert.

"I don't know," replied Minty Lou. "He's under the table. I'm going back to school." She went, to be patched up by the second-grade teacher, who kept a few bandages and supplies in her desk. To Teacher's questions, she only said she had been in a fight.

"That's a knife cut," exclaimed Teacher, scandalized.

"It doesn't hurt much," said Minty Lou.

Left to herself, Grandma would undoubtedly have whipped Minty Lou till the blood came. Gordie was not dead, but he had to be taken to the clinic and a nasty wound stitched up. Joe mended the broken chair, but there was nothing to be done about the plate, while the landlord would be in no hurry to patch the hole in the wall. Luckily for Minty Lou, Tom and Bert had found Gordie with the knife still in his hand. Tom thought this was not fair fighting and said so.

"You let the kid alone, Ma," he ordered with most unusual decision. "It was Gordie's fault."

Grandma glared at him; but she was after a fashion a just woman, and she knew that Tom was right. She did not raise a hand against Minty Lou on this occasion, but she could not forgive her. That brat had half killed her poor Gordie! Min

was bad all through, and Grandma had had
enough of her. She would not keep her.

"You aiming to send her to her other grandma?"
asked Arlene at the end of a tirade. The question
stopped Grandma in her tracks. She darted a sus-
picious look at Minty Lou, who was wiping the

supper dishes. She need not have bothered to worry! The brat didn't care!

Actually Minty Lou had not been listening, once it was clear that Grandma would not whip her. But even if she had heard the suggestion, she would not have liked it. Grandma Minty had been sweet and kind, but then so had Grandma Payson in those far-off days when she had been too little to know that grownups naturally liked to hurt. Besides, Momma had cried about the way they lived in Cambridge and had not wanted Grandma Minty to go back. She and Grandpa were very poor, Momma had said.

Minty Lou now knew about being poor. It meant no proper bathroom and dresses in pawn and holes in her stockings and too tight shoes. It also meant hard work and no pay with people calling you a burden and blaming you when the meat went off or when there was mold on the bread and too little for supper. Decidedly she did not want to be poorer than ever.

Worse still, there was something bad about being poor in Cambridge, which was not the same as being poor in Baltimore. It was something to do with the hospital, with Momma's button, with having what Grandma called "git-up-and-go." Momma would not have gone back there, not for anything you could give her. She had said so. Someday when she was big enough, Minty Lou was going to the hospital, where they would remember Momma and give her a job. She couldn't do that if she went back to Cambridge.

Arlene was surprised when her ma dropped the subject of getting rid of Minty Lou. It did not occur to her that Ma was worried lest those Hayeses should try to get their hands on the insurance, a little of which remained, a tiny cushion against old age and sickness. For though there were jobs in Baltimore for those that had git-up-and-go, there were no kinfolk and children were apt to drift away. When she thought of it, Grandma had a sick feeling about her old age.

Secretly Grandma racked her brains. There was the orphanage, but she did not think it would take in Minty Lou without inquiring about the insurance. She could not quite turn the kid into the street. The neighbors, the church, and even Grandma herself would be scandalized at such a thing. Why "they" might even put her in the jailhouse for what she done. Grandma shuddered at the thought.

Grandma felt baffled, but it was not her way to leave a subject for long. Pretty soon she could hardly see Minty Lou without screaming that she would not have that brat in her house with her savage temper, not after the way she nearly killed poor Gordie. But after a few days of this, something happened which made all yelling at Minty Lou practically useless, presenting Grandma with a further problem.

The White Lady

ABOUT THREE MONTHS EARLIER, Grandma had found a Saturday job for Minty Lou, cleaning for a lady who had a big house and needed help. Minty Lou was very willing because she would have been cleaning all Saturday in any case. The lady offered lunch and a whole dollar, besides a chance to get away from Grandma.

What Minty Lou did not reckon on was that any lady who would hire a little girl to do her work was bound to be one that older girls would not work for. Mrs. Murch — her name was Murchison, but Minty Lou could never get around it — was a bully. Her favorite phrase in giving orders was, "Don't you dare!"

"Clean out that cabinet," she'd say, "and don't you dare drop my good china!"

"Fetch a bucket of water, and don't you dare spill on my floor!"

Minty Lou did her best to be careful, but Mrs. Murch was always hustling, sneaking up behind

to see if she was working as hard as she ought.
Mrs. Murch was free with her hands, too. On
that first Saturday, Minty Lou's round cheeks felt
sore from being slapped. At the end of the day
when she asked for her money, Mrs. Murch only
glared. "I pay it to your grandma."

When she got home that evening, Minty Lou
had the nerve to tell Grandma that she did not
like going out to work! But Grandma had gone to
work at six, and what was good enough for her
was surely all right for a kid that was thrown as
a burden on her grandma.

"When Gordie earns a dollar," insisted Minty
Lou sulkily, "he gets to keep it." She was not yet
quite at the stage where she did not argue.

If Grandma had known a painless way of ex-
tracting money from Gordie, she would have used
it; but she was not going to be pinned down to
explaining her methods to Minty Lou. She cuffed
her instead, ordering her to shut her mouth. She
was going back to Mrs. Murch and might as well
make up her mind to that.

After this, Saturdays became days of dread.
What was worse, Minty Lou could never manage
to get Mrs. Murch out of her head the rest of the
week. She had not before this time met many
white people to speak to. The lady in the shop,
whose little girl had a stocking doll called Molly,
had always greeted her kindly and had been generous with bits of candy. The rent man had laughed

at her chatter. On one occasion he had given her a
nickel for being a cute kid. Mrs. Murch simply did
not like colored people, and she was always making
it clear.

Up to now, Minty Lou had never bothered
about white people being richer and more power-
ful than ordinary folks. When Momma had explained that this was always so, Minty Lou had
asked why in the same spirit as that in which she
had asked why the sun always rose in the East.
She had not really listened to the answer, nor had
it occurred to her to be sorry she was black.

Mrs. Murch loomed over her, a big, stout
woman who would not let anything she did be
right, not because she was an orphan and had to
earn her keep, but because she was black. Something inside Minty Lou did not want to put up
with feeling degraded.

This might have been something she had learned
from Momma, so proud of her job, so big, so con-
fident, so able. It might have been partly because
she was named for Harriet Tubman, who had
rescued three hundred folk from slavery. Minty
Lou was too young to wonder why she had the
feeling that, though she might be a burden on
Grandma, she would not put up with being what
Mrs. Murch called her.

She had no way of fighting back except by
hating; but it was not enough to hate Mrs. Murch
the way she did Grandma. She hated her because

she was a white person, and she started to shrink
into herself when she passed a white man brushing
arrogantly through the colored quarter. She was
glad to keep out of sight of Grandma's rent man,
who talked tough to Grandma and made her pawn
something if she was so much as a few cents behind

on Saturdays. She listened to stories that she heard from other kids about white people who were every bit as bad as Mrs. Murch. This did not surprise her because everyone who had power was cruel with it. Bullied and helpless, but not quite cowed, Minty Lou bared her teeth like a little animal, waiting her chance to teach the world that they were sharp. The second-grade teacher had not been so far out about that knife.

The Saturday after her big fight with Gordie, Minty Lou was still upset from the excitement and from the terrible rows that had followed with Grandma. Perhaps for that reason Mrs. Murch seemed worse than usual. She was pushed about and "don't-you-dared" till she started to cry. Mrs. Murch slapped her and told her not to snivel, but to hurry up and make the biscuits for lunch. "And don't you dare not to wash your hands before you start them!"

Minty Lou still sniffed a bit, but she went to the tap and washed her hands, which were just as clean as those of Mrs. Murch. She climbed on a chair to get down the mixing bowl. She collected the flour, the soda, the milk, the mixing spoon, the pastry board, and rolling pin on the kitchen table. It all took time because she was unable to reach things. Mrs. Murch was standing by the stove stirring soup with a big ladle and telling Minty Lou she was slow.

Minty Lou brought the chair back to the table

to stand on in order to reach into the mixing bowl. Mr. Murch was in for lunch, and there were two or three grown children around on Saturdays — she did not quite know how many because she seldom went in the front of the house. This meant a fairly big batch of biscuits. Grandma or Mrs. Murch had shown her how to make them, and usually she did all right. Today her nerves were on edge. She kept stealing glances at Mrs. Murch to see if she were watching, but Mrs. Murch was putting a pinch of something in the pot.

It was difficult to turn the dough out onto the board for rolling because the huge kitchen implements were all too big for her hands. However, she got it there successfully and reached for the rolling pin to dust it with flour. This was big and clumsy, too. It escaped from her fingers and fell on the floor with a telltale clatter. Horrified, Minty Lou glanced at Mrs. Murch, but that lady was tasting the soup and did not seem to notice. She scrambled down to pick up the rolling pin. She knew she ought to wash it, but Mrs. Murch would want to know why. It looked quite clean.

She got back on to her chair and dusted it with flour. She was just going to press it into the dough when Mrs. Murch, who had been waiting the whole time to catch her out, turned on her in a rage. "You dirty little beast! Take that!" She aimed a blow at Minty Lou with the ladle which caught her on the ear and knocked her down.

For a moment or two Minty Lou lay limply
where she fell. When she came to her senses, Mrs.
Murch was standing over her shouting, "Don't you
dare do that dirty thing again ever! Don't you
dare!" The frightening thing was that though
Minty Lou could see that Mrs. Murch was yelling,
all she could hear was a thready sound from a
great distance. Then it faded away altogether in
the middle of "Don't you dare!"

"Get up!" cried Mrs. Murch. "Don't you lay
there pretending to be hurt! Get up at once!"
Minty Lou could see her mouth opening and
shutting, but she could not hear one word. Her
head ached terribly, and she was shivering all
over.

Mrs. Murch yanked her up by the arm and
plumped her into a chair, saying something else.
Minty Lou said, "I can't hear." She started crying.

Mrs. Murch actually brought her a glass of
water, but she pushed it away. She was sobbing
hysterically, but only partly from the pain in her
head. A terrifying silence walled her off from the
rest of the world. "I can't hear anything," she
wailed. "I just can't hear."

Mrs. Murch went away to fetch Mr. Murch,
who stared at her, his pink bald forehead puckered
into a frown. He shouted at her, too, but she could
not hear him. He said something to Mrs. Murch,
who brought her some soup. She drank a couple

of mouthfuls and began to calm down, though she still shivered.

Mr. Murch bent over and tried to pat her on the arm, but she shrank away. He felt in his pocket and took out a silver dollar. Then, mouthing the words so that she could understand, he said, "Run home and lie down for a bit. You'll soon be better." He put his face down close to hers, "*And don't you dare make trouble!* Understand?" She nodded, his breath hot on her face as he pressed the dollar into her palm.

Mrs. Murch pulled her up, led her to the door, and pushed her out.

When Minty Lou got back again to Grandma's, she was in such a state that something had to be done. Grandma bustled into her street clothes and took her to the clinic. After a long time there was a doctor, pink and bald like Mr. Murch. He tried to make Minty Lou hear, but he was unable to. He asked a few questions, but she was not going to give him a chance to make things worse. She shook her head. He talked to Grandma then, but Grandma was not anxious to explain how she had hired out Minty Lou to Mrs. Murch. Besides, she knew better than to try and get white people into trouble. What was the use? "She had a fall," Grandma said.

The doctor did not pursue the matter. Perhaps he realized that he would not get the truth, or perhaps he did not care. The kid was deaf, and she would either get better or not. If she did not, further diagnosis would be needed and perhaps an operation. He told Grandma so, although he knew perfectly that she neither could nor would afford to have anything done. It was out of his hands.

Minty Lou did not get better. She had horrible headaches, and she could not hear a word that anyone said. Teacher said she ought to go to deaf school, but it turned out there was no room in the one for colored kids. She had to go to school somewhere, and she was not a nuisance in class. In fact, she was quite clever at understanding what Teacher said.

Minty Lou lived alone in a private world for several weeks. This had the advantage that she did not have to listen to Grandma any longer and she did not have to go back to Mrs. Murch. All the same, it was like being locked into a sound-proof glass box, alone with your thoughts. She simply brooded daylong, miserable and angry, never distracted by a laugh or a joke at school or by listening to Teacher. Most of the time, sunk in gloom, she did not know what she was thinking. Often she was frightened because people came up behind without her hearing.

Grandma told Arlene she had more than enough of that brat. You had only to look at her to see

she was vicious. Poor Gordie was careful enough
to leave her alone, but you could see her jump
and snarl if he came near her unexpectedly. She
did her housework, it was true, since there was no
need for anything but signs about that. All the
same, she was dangerous to have around with
that look in her eye!

Grandma said this sort of thing because deep
down in her mind she was frightened of being
saddled with a deaf and crazy kid that could not
earn. What was going to happen if Minty Lou
became a burden forever? Like the swimmer on
whom a drowning man has fastened himself,
Grandma was fighting for her life.

"I won't keep her," she declared for the thou-
sandth time. "I won't keep that brat any longer."

"Then where's she to go?" asked Joe, glancing
uneasily at Minty Lou dishing up the beans. He
could never get used to the feeling of talking her
over in her presence.

"The orphanage wouldn't take her," Arlene
said. "Not the way she is. She ought rightly to
be in one of them homes for crazy kids."

Grandma nodded. They'd been through this a
thousand times and got no further.

"I was thinking," Arlene said reflectively, "just
thinking, mind . . . Would Aunt Helen take
her?"

"Aunt *Helen!*" Grandma's spoon, poised over

the beans she was helping, hesitated. "That's fifty-three and hasn't had no children and never wanted none! You're crazy, Arlene!"

"She could afford to, couldn't she?" Arlene said.

Grandma sniffed. "Oh, she could afford to, with Elmer working steady and her having those jobs with white folks, and the both of them with no one else to keep! I guess you never so much as been in her house, Arlene."

"Never was asked that I remember," Arlene agreed. "Not even when we married, was we, Joe?"

Joe shook his head.

"If she's too high and mighty to notice you, Arlene, that's her own brother's kid, why for would she take the brat that's no more than Jim's daughter? She never did nary a thing to help when we first come to town."

"I know . . ." Arlene hesitated. "Didn't you say as how she got religion? Ain't she ashamed not to act Christian? Won't her church tell her she got to take that kid on?"

"I dunno," Grandma reflected. "Maybe you got something there, Arlene. It's sure worth trying."

Aunt Helen it was.

The Miracle

MINTY LOU was moved over to Aunt Helen's one Saturday afternoon, carrying a brown paper parcel with what was left of her clothing. Arlene had written down for her where she was going, and Grandma fulfilled her last duty by taking her there on the streetcar. "Acting dumb," she summed up on her return. "Wasn't about to speak to Aunt Helen. Never a word of thanks for all I done."

"She had the earache," Arlene replied indifferently. "It was one of her bad days."

"Never had no good days if you ask me," Grandma snapped. "The sulky brat! There belongs to be a spoon in that box in the corner. D'you see it, Arlene? Is you and Joe in to supper tonight? It's beans."

Minty Lou hardly knew where she was. She had no impression of Aunt Helen because the jerky progress of the streetcar had set up agony inside her head. She sat in a corner, hand over her ear, and wished she were dead. Luckily Aunt Helen, whatever else she might be like, was efficient. She wasted no time trying to get acquainted, but found a rag, dipped it in hot water, wrung it out and gave it to Minty Lou to hold against her ear. She took the parcel of clothes and went away. Presently she came back to lead Minty Lou upstairs. Right next the bathroom was a neat little bedroom with a cot bedstead in it, cheap but solid, made up with sheets. Minty Lou's only whole nightgown lay across it.

It felt wonderful to get into a real bed. Aunt Helen produced a rubber hot-water bottle, a present from one of her ladies who preferred a good old stone crock to these new inventions. Minty Lou sank gratefully back and let warmth penetrate her aching head. It did a lot of good, and after a time she actually dozed.

Aunt Helen woke her up after dark, appearing with a candle and supper on a tray with a crocheted doily. Instead of beans, there was a potato pie with bits of chicken in the sauce under the crust. There was not much of it, but she did not like to ask for more in case Aunt Helen might think she was shamming sick. It was delicious though. Aunt Helen renewed the hot water in the rubber bottle and took the tray away, and also the candle.

Minty Lou did not sleep till late, but she was warm enough in bed for the first time that winter. She was lying on a mattress, and the hot bottle felt comfortable against her head. Toward morning she dropped off.

One of the difficulties about being deaf was that the noises of the household getting up did not arouse her. When somebody shook her awake, she thought it was Grandma and put up a hand to shield her head, glaring resentfully into the strange face that was bending over her.

Aunt Helen looked at her without joy. She was already in her best for church, a black dress several inches longer than the fashion, so that it swept the floor, with a white starched collar and cuffs. It was stylish just now to wear hobble skirts, but Aunt Helen's were wide and ample, giving her an almost monumental appearance. She was not tall, but she held herself stiffly as she regarded Minty Lou with the expression of one determined to make the best of an unwelcome job. Once more, she made no attempt to communicate, but merely put down the same tray with the doily, which had on it a bowl of oatmeal with molasses and a glass of milk. She collected the hot-water bottle and came back with fresh water in it, which Minty Lou took as an order to stay in bed. She frowned a little when she saw the breakfast bowl was already empty; but instead of saying anything about it, she picked up the tray and, mouthing her words clearly, remarked, "We . . . are . . . going . . . to . . . church. Understand?"

Minty Lou said, "Yes, ma'am."

"Your . . . lunch . . . is . . . in . . . the . . .
kitchen."

She did not bother to explain where she and
Uncle Elmer were having lunch or when they
would get home, but went out closing the door
while Minty Lou was getting up courage to ask
for another bowl of oatmeal.

Minty Lou lay back in bed and looked around
her. The wallpaper had a lavender stripe splashed
over with bunches of lilac tied with purple ribbon.
Most of the opposite wall was taken up with an
enormous dark wardrobe with curly feet and fret-
work top, its mirror carefully pasted over with
brown paper. Crowded into a corner was an
elderly dark-green painted bureau. The floor,
whose paint looked recent, was a glossy dark
brown. Green plush framed the window, which
was also covered with lace curtains. The effect was
grand, if a trifle dark; but it made Minty Lou
and her cot bed seem out of place. Minty Lou later
discovered that Aunt Helen got castoffs from her
white ladies, while Uncle Elmer, who spent most
of his spare time in the cellar, repaired broken
legs or touched up worn pieces with sticky brown
polish. The wardrobe which dominated Minty
Lou's room was one of his failures, since the door
swung open and the drawer below it jammed.

Presently she got up because she was still hungry
and wanted to see what there was for lunch in the
kitchen. There was bread and salami. The icebox

on the back porch was locked, but Minty Lou
found the breadbox and cut herself a slice as thick
as she dared. Feeling better, she began to explore
the house.

Aunt Helen's house downstairs was rather like
Momma's, except more splendid. Instead of the
front door opening into the parlor, it gave on to
a vestibule tiled and wainscoted in red and yellow
marble. This was lighted through the front door,
which had a panel of beautiful red-and-green
glass with a flower design. The parlor was im-
pressive, too, with green plush furniture, red
velvet curtains, a velvet drape on the mantelpiece,
flowered rug, lace-covered tables, and a variety
of pink vases with pictures on them. Over the
mantel hung the picture of a lady whose nightgown was coming loose. She was clinging with
both arms to a cross planted on a rock surrounded
by the most tremendous waves which were trying
to wash the lady away. It was called, "The Soul's
Refuge."

Minty Lou gazed at "The Soul's Refuge" while
she let her thoughts dwell on Aunt Helen and
Uncle Elmer in church. She had never been to
church or Sunday school since Pop and Momma
died. In the beginning she had said her prayers
at night when she was at Grandma's, but not lately.
There was no one she wanted God to bless and
nothing to thank for. Even God wouldn't give her
Momma and Poppa again. She understood that.

But the long rest and the relief of not being with
Grandma had aroused a faint desire to be herself.
She did not suppose she was going to like Aunt
Helen, or anyone else ever. It would be stupid to
be so soft. But it might be a good thing to hear
what was said.

"The Soul's Refuge" stirred in Minty Lou a
memory of that party dress that she had prayed
so hard for and had got — even if she did only
wear it once. She wondered if God was waiting for
her to pray before the deafness went away. She
reflected. She could listen to Teacher. She might
even play house or jacks with the kids at recess.
She might . . . Dumb misery broke like an ab-
scess, and she was conscious of a tremendous feeling of relief. She wanted something! With all of
her, not just now and then, she wanted to hear.

She tried a prayer at once, but it seemed to make
no difference. She decided she had better go on
for a while because big presents, Momma used
to say, took a mighty lot of praying. Meanwhile,
there was the hot bottle for her earache. She
fetched it into the kitchen and filled it from the
kettle. She wondered if Aunt Helen didn't want
her parlor sat in just like Grandma. It didn't smell
used.

Aunt Helen and Uncle Elmer came back looking tired. Uncle Elmer, whom she hadn't seen
before, had a lot of age onto him. His hair was
nearly white, and he moved with a slow shuffle. He

patted her cheek smiling shyly, but she only stared back at him with dark suspicion.

Supper was soon ready. There were sausage patties and fried bread. That is, Uncle Elmer had two patties on a slice of fried bread, and Aunt Helen had the same. The moment Minty Lou saw her own plate, she went hot all over because there was just the sausage on it, but no bread. After the blessing, Uncle Elmer noticed and asked a question. Minty Lou could see that Aunt Helen was explaining how she had stolen bread right out of the breadbox. She drooped over her plate and would not look at them.

After a time, Aunt Helen brought in cold rice pudding, so evenly divided onto the three plates that she might easily have counted every grain. Minty Lou tried not to finish first, but she was unable to eat slowly. There was another blessing, and then Aunt Helen showed her how to do the washing up.

Next morning there was another school with a tired teacher who never found out that Minty Lou was deaf. She gave her name and told where she came from. Then she sat at the back for the rest of the day. Unknown to her, a few more forms began in their uninterested way to trace her fortunes by moving from one school file to another school file; but since they came to rest in the right spot, they raised no fuss.

Two nights later, Minty Lou dreamed that she

heard a noise. It woke her up. She sat bolt upright in bed, her heart beating madly, but the usual silence surrounded her. She stole to the window and parted the curtains to look out. Below her stretched the sloping roof of the kitchen and a tiny yard, giving onto a back alley. All the houses opposite were dark except one, which was the back of a restaurant facing onto a main street. Its garbage pails stood almost across from Aunt Helen's, visible in the light of a sickly streetlamp. A man in a white apron was bending over to pick up the lid of one which he had dropped. Impatiently he crammed it back with a movement which must have made a clatter, but she could not hear it. He went back inside and could be seen to bang his door. A black-and-white cat dropped from the roof of a lean-to shed onto the lid of the garbage pail to sniff it over. Minty Lou said another prayer before going back to bed.

A second week began. Aunt Helen did not believe in pampering children, and she kept Minty Lou very busy with the housework. There was real relief, however, in not being pestered by Gordie and the boys; while it was almost a pleasure to wash that beautiful marble and polish those knobs. Aunt Helen's standards were a great deal higher than Grandma's, and she looked sour when she found fault. On the other hand, she was clever and patient at making Minty Lou understand; and she seemed willing to give her a little time to settle in. Uncle Elmer never tried to speak, but he still smiled when he came up from the cellar for meals or met Minty Lou on the landing. Minty Lou made no effort to like either of them, but she was grateful for not being pushed around. It would be restful at Aunt Helen's even when she could hear.

On Thursday of the following week, Minty
Lou woke again to a sound. It was a scraping noise
which seemed familiar, though she was uncertain
whether it was in the house, or only in her head.
It came again, accompanied by a clatter. Aunt
Helen was moving the big hot-water pan to the
side of the stove in the kitchen! She was clattering
the pitchers which she filled and brought upstairs
for washing and shaving. Uncle Elmer pulled the
plug in the bathroom, and Minty Lou heard the
water come rushing down. He came out and
banged the door. Minty Lou leaped wildly out of
bed and tore onto the landing to fling her arms
about his waist. "Uncle Elmer! Uncle Elmer! I
can *hear!*"

It was a glorious moment, the first second of
wild happiness since Momma had died, the first
spontaneous gesture. Uncle Elmer patted her head
and cleared his throat. He was excited himself, but
he was scared of children and did not know what
to say. He was also worried lest Helen come up
and find Minty Lou in her nightgown. Helen's
religion had given her strong views about what
was decent.

"Er-well," he said in a quavery voice which
sounded even older than he looked to Minty Lou.
"Er-well, that's right good news! It surely is!" His
eloquence dried up as he cocked an ear uneasily
for Helen, who would be bringing up his shaving
water any minute. Awkwardly he kissed the top

of Minty Lou's head. "I sure am happy for you! Er . . . yes, indeed, I sure am! Best run and dress, and then you can surprise your aunt. I won't tell her." He put a finger to his lips as a sign of conspiracy and gave her a little push toward her bedroom door. "Go on now, run away!"

Minty Lou was not dashed by his awkwardness. In fact, it suited her better at this time than a warm response. She did not want to be cuddled. But the sudden miracle had floated her back to the days people had called her a cute kid. A dog barked in the alley, and she heard it. A barrow man was shouting vegetables in the front street, no doubt hoping to catch housewives before they went to work. The whole world was alive, and Minty Lou skipped on the floor.

Aunt Helen smiled all over her face and put an extra spoonful of oatmeal in Minty Lou's bowl by mistake. She did not even take it out when she saw what she had done, just tut-tutted gently, shaking her head at herself.

"I prayed for you to get well," she said in a syrupy voice.

"So did I," agreed Uncle Elmer.

"And so did I," cried Minty Lou, laughing from sheer joy. "I prayed all the time!"

"Let us give thanks," Aunt Helen said, showing an example by plumping down on her knees on the kitchen floor. They all knelt while Aunt Helen said a long prayer, and Uncle Elmer cried "Amen"

and "Hallelujah!" Minty Lou's heart nearly burst
with joy because God cared about her, which she
told herself was better by far than Aunt Helen
caring, or Teacher, or Grandma, or any of the
uninterested people she had to live with. It gave
her a bit of the old days back, a sense of being
somebody special. Now that she had a real bureau,
she had not often bothered to put on Momma's
button; but this morning she had pinned it under
her dress because she did not want to talk about
Momma to Aunt Helen. She felt it while Aunt
Helen's prayer went on and on.

Aunt Helen's prayer was a little strange, and
it certainly sounded as though Aunt Helen herself
had done all the praying and persuaded God to
notice Minty Lou. Still, nothing mattered much,
not even when Aunt Helen, dusting off her skirt
as she got up, remarked, "That floor's disgraceful!
You'd better give it a good scrubbing this afternoon." Minty Lou's spirits were not damped.
Before the kitchen floor, there would be school.

Even the tired teacher noticed Minty Lou that
day. "That's quite a cute kid," she said in her limp
way at recess, "that new one that just started up
follow-my-leader."

"What's her name?"

"One of them double names. I don't rightly
remember."

"Shabby looking," commented the other teacher
sourly.

On the Monday that she first went to school,
Aunt Helen had frowned over Minty Lou's appearance and said that it was disgraceful and
immodest. It was true that her dresses were over
her knees and there were gaps in the buttons which
ought to have fastened them behind. Aunt Helen
said it was indecent for a Christian girl to be seen
in such garments and would not let her go to
church on the following Sunday. The day before,
on her half day off, she had made a visit to a large
cheap clothing store and come home laden. The
underwear she produced was of the plainest sort
and clearly selected for hard wear. She had bought
two dresses, neither of them pretty; but she said
they needed altering and seemed to be planning
something at the neck. Minty Lou had hopes of
a frill.

These dresses were not yet done, but everything
looked hopeful on this most glorious of days.
Uncle Elmer almost split his face in a grin when
he got home from work, and he said, "Still *hear,*
eh?" chuckling at his pun. Aunt Helen grudgingly
approved of the kitchen floor. One way and another, Minty Lou found courage to do what she
had not dared ever since the episode of the stolen
slice of bread. In secret she had discovered that
the bakery which she passed on the way to school
sold yesterday's doughnuts three for a nickel. She
still had Mr. Murch's dollar, so that she had been
able to fill up. By now the dollar was half gone,

but everything would be all right, she felt sure.
She said boldly at supper, "Can't I have more to
eat? I'm still hungry."

A heavy frown clamped down over Aunt Helen's
face. "Greed is a sin, and you have had sufficient."
She removed the plates and came back with three
pieces of gingerbread hot from the oven. Minty
Lou's was the smallest, not so small that Uncle
Elmer would notice, but small enough to say, "You
must be punished."

"That child needs discipline," remarked Aunt
Helen sourly, while Minty Lou was doing the
washing up. "Sulks when she's spoken to, just like
her Grandma Ellen Payson said. A single word'll
set her off."

Uncle Elmer never contradicted Aunt Helen.
He said vaguely, "Er-yes?"

"And she's come to the right place to get discipline," added Aunt Helen with relish. "I know
my duty, none better."

There was a gleam in her eye which expressed
satisfaction at the idea of teaching Minty Lou a
useful lesson. Uncle Elmer stirred uneasily. He
did admire Aunt Helen, but there was no doubt
that she loved power.

"D'you think she might've been downright
hungry? Er-well . . ." His voice trailed off.

"She eats as much as you," Aunt Helen's tone
was sharp. "And you a grown man! Don't start
that nonsense, Elmer."

It passed through Uncle Elmer's mind that his own appetite had fallen off over the years, but he dared not say so. The whole question of his diet was dangerous ground. The chief object of his life had long been to conceal from Aunt Helen the sinful glass of beer he drank with his lunch. Experience told him that the only way to keep anything from her was never to touch on the subject at all. He said, "Er-well . . ." and pottered off down cellar.

The Brothers and Sisters

AUNT HELEN watched Minty Lou with a secret enjoyment which she explained to herself as determination to do what was right by a stubborn child. She made her portions at meals a little smaller, telling herself it was her duty to make it quite clear that sulking did not pay. Minty Lou did what she was told and said, "Yes, ma'am," when spoken to, but her manner of looking at Aunt Helen was almost as offensive as her fixed stare at Grandma. Even Uncle Elmer, though he was used to eating in silence, began to find meals oppressive. He gave up smiling at Minty Lou and spent still more time in the cellar.

Minty Lou quite made up her mind that grownups were either indifferent like Teacher and Arlene, or they were cruel like Grandma and Mrs. Murch. Aunt Helen was one of the cruel ones, quiet though she was. Uncle Elmer did not care. One could expect no better, but God at least did care. Her miracle gave her a warm feeling which did not wear off, even though she still had bouts of earache. When Aunt Helen talked about going to church, Minty Lou's "Yes, ma'am" concealed pleasure at the thought of the familiar hymns and a Sunday school teacher.

For a couple of nights Aunt Helen had been sewing to fix up one of the new dresses for church. She did not show what she was doing, and Minty Lou would not ask. All the same, it was exciting to be going to wear a new dress with white buttons and something white at the neck. Some of the kids at school had sneered at her clothes.

When she went to bed on Saturday night, the dress was not ready. Aunt Helen promised that it would be hanging in her wardrobe the following morning. She woke when it was still dark and lay awake thinking about the new dress and going to church again. At first light she dropped off, only waking when Uncle Elmer banged the bathroom door, which was her signal to get up and wash. She slid out of bed, pulled the creaking door of the wardrobe wide, and stared in.

It had been a dark blue dress, quite plain except for a V-neck and little white buttons on the sleeves, which were skimpy, betraying its cheapness. Aunt Helen had filled up the V-neck by the simple process of tacking inside it a piece of old sheet which she happened to have by her. She had taken the buttons off and lengthened the sleeves with tight black cuffs. Finally she had lengthened the skirt to the ground by adding to it a broad black band made out of a petticoat which had seen its best days and been retired from service.

It did not pay to be soft. If Minty Lou had cherished no hopes, the shock might have been borne. As it was, she burst into tears of rage, snatched the dress off its hanger and tried to tear the black band off; but it was sewn too tightly.

Aunt Helen called up to tell her to wash before the hot water was cold; but Minty Lou, who had looked all around for her old dresses and found them missing, would not stir. Aunt Helen sailed upstairs with the inner satisfaction of one prepared to do unpleasant duty. She found Minty Lou in bed and the dress on the floor.

"Pick that dress up," she ordered in her cold way, "and put it on."

"I won't," howled Minty Lou in a burst of tears. "Everybody would point at me in the street. I'd rather wear my old ones."

"I threw them out," retorted Aunt Helen firmly. "They weren't even fit for the rag bag. In future you'll put on what's proper for a modest Christian girl. There'll be no necks, nor legs and elbows showing out of sinful vanity or worse. Temptations of the Devil, that's what these modern fashions are. We weren't put in this world to think of our garments."

A thought so horrible struck Minty Lou that she even stopped crying. "Not to *school!* I can't wear that dress to school as well as church."

"What's good enough for church is good enough for school. You can't sin all week long and be clothed in righteousness on Sundays. Those that aren't waiting for the Last Trumpet go into the fire."

"All the kids will laugh," cried Minty Lou in a wail. "They'll point at me and call me a witch."

"A Christian needn't pay no mind," retorted Aunt Helen, closing the argument. "I'm not about to have it said that in my house there is pampering of worldly vanity."

"I won't," screamed Minty Lou. She threw herself face down in the bed and lay there sobbing, pounding the pillow with her fists.

Efficient as always, Aunt Helen went to her own room for a belt of Uncle Elmer's, twitched the bedclothes off Minty Lou, and started to thrash her. Minty Lou screamed.

Uncle Elmer came stumbling upstairs at a run. He seized Aunt Helen by the arm and twisted the belt out of her hand. "You're not to do it," he shouted at her. "I can't stand it, see?"

Aunt Helen turned about to face him. For an instant, they glared at each other, panting slightly. Aunt Helen was the first to recover herself.

"Now, Elmer," she said in her cool way, "what do you know about bringing up a girl? She needs a lesson, and I'm about to teach it to her once and for all." Her eyes were shining as though what she had been doing was exciting.

Uncle Elmer looked at the floor. "I just can't stand it," he mumbled. "You don't lay a finger on her, see? Or I'll . . ." He still had her wrist in his hand, and he tightened his grip. The strap was swinging in his other hand.

There was silence for a minute except for the sobs of Minty Lou. Aunt Helen shrugged her shoulders philosophically. She knew Elmer, mild as milk most of the time — but there were moments when he turned obstinate. In any case, there were other ways of teaching lessons.

"Very well," she agreed curtly, "but those that won't obey don't get to eat. Unless I see you in half an hour to breakfast, you'll stay here locked in your room with no lunch either. Make up your mind." She took Uncle Elmer with her and swept out.

Minty Lou lay there desperately sobbing. The belt had hurt, but it had frightened her as well. She had tried to stand up for herself, but she was not big enough to do it. If Aunt Helen wanted to dress her like an old witch, she would have to put up with being laughed at. Her difficulty was to face the moment of putting that dress on. Presently, however, she panicked at the thought of missing breakfast and lunch, just as Aunt Helen had been sure she would. She crammed herself into the detested garment, roughly rinsed her face in the bathroom, and clattered down into the kitchen swollen with crying.

Aunt Helen had her eye on the kitchen clock as she said with satisfaction, "I told you, Elmer! You'd better believe that I can manage her." She looked Minty Lou over. "Do up that button at the neck and don't come down half dressed another time."

"It's too tight," protested Minty Lou in a sullen mumble.

Aunt Helen whisked her around, shaking her a little, and did the button firmly up. "You've got five minutes for breakfast," she said. "It's cold by now."

Minty Lou choked down a sob and started to eat. Aunt Helen was packing a sandwich lunch in a basket. It was a bigger lunch than the weekday one, with cold tea in a bottle, an apple apiece, gingerbread, two kinds of sandwich, and a substantial wedge of cheese. Minty Lou stared blankly at this generous feast until Aunt Helen told her sharply not to sit dawdling.

"Take your bowl across to the sink, and then get your coat on. You'll have to make do with the old one this year, and that blue bonnet." The bonnet was one which Momma had made out of velvet and lined with pale blue silk. Luckily it was dark blue on the outside, so that Aunt Helen, though she muttered over the velvet and the lining, had

not replaced it. The shabby coat covered most of
the new dress, leaving the black part flapping
around her ankles.

Church turned out to be a vacant store in a dingy
street. Across its curtained windows somebody had
painted on the glass in staggering letters BROTHERS
OF CHRIST. As an afterthought, he had added AND
SISTERS, cramping the words to fit into the space
below BROTHERS. Inside, the preacher, whose
smooth black face was shining as though he pol-
ished it for Sundays, was helping a stout lady in
a black dress like a tent and a high black turban to
take her place before a harmonium so small that
it seemed almost unfair for her to play on it. Seeing Aunt Helen, he bustled forward, hand out-
stretched.

"Sister Robbins! Always the first! The Lord has
indeed blessed you this week! And Brother Robins
also."

"Glory, glory! I felt the Power," responded
Aunt Helen in throbbing tones.

"I know it's so! I know it's so!" agreed Uncle
Elmer.

"So this is our orphan child!" The preacher
picked up Minty Lou's small hand and held it en-
closed in his own while she dropped him a curtsy.
"So this is the little deaf girl that your prayers
have healed! Great is the favor of God towards
His faithful people."

"Glory be to God!" cried the fat lady in a reso-

nant voice, wriggling herself around upon the harmonium stool to stare at Minty Lou.

At this moment two more ladies arrived, closely
followed by a faded couple with five children of
varying ages. Minty Lou eyed them, resentful because the dresses of the girls, though longer than
the fashion, were a good deal off the floor, merely
giving the impression that they thought they had
reached the age when girls' dresses did lengthen.

The preacher hurried away with further greet-
ings, while Aunt Helen was surrounded by people
who wanted to stare at Minty Lou and touch her.
Could she actually hear as well as ever? Wasn't
she grateful to God and to Sister Robbins, which
was Aunt Helen.

The only possible answer to such questions was
a "Yes, ma'am" and a curtsy. Minty Lou per-
formed her part, but with swelling resentment.
The ladies did not even stop to listen to her. Everyone's interest was in the startling fashion in which
God had answered the prayers of Aunt Helen.
Her devotion in adopting an orphan child was
surely a lesson to other poor sinners. The Lord had
blessed her for it. He surely had! Everybody
wanted to know whether Sister Robbins had felt
the Power within her.

"I felt the Lord!" Aunt Helen replied over and
over again. "Great is His Power!"

"I know it's so! I know it's so!" repeated Uncle
Elmer, who seemed to have adopted this useful

phrase as a comment on what the Brothers and
Sisters of Christ might happen to say. It was sorely
needed because the Brothers and Sisters were terrible talkers who looked on silence as a sign of
faint religion.

Minty Lou's scowl deepened. She had been a
little impressed by the preacher, but all these ladies
around Aunt Helen were different. They were taking away the warm feeling that God had cared
specially, and they were giving it to Aunt Helen
instead. Besides they were staring at her as if at
the organ grinder's monkey, cute because she could
hear, but for no other reason.

"Couldn't you hear anything?" they screamed
at her over the noise.

"No, ma'am!"

"It's a miracle, Sister Robbins!" they cried,
turning back to Aunt Helen.

"I felt the Power!" Aunt Helen agreed.

Minty Lou hated them all, even down to the
scattered children, who drew into whispering
clumps as their mothers surrounded Aunt Helen.
"I won't sing with these people," she vowed to
herself. She looked around the old store with nothing pretty in it, and she muttered, "This isn't a
church."

She might just possibly have got over her sulks
and joined in if the service had turned out to be
anything like what she was used to. The preacher
did start by praying, but he seemed to slide into

preaching almost at once, looking hotter as he went on and thumping his table. Minty Lou gave a positive start when Aunt Helen bounced up to yell, "Hallelujah!" right in the middle of a sentence. The preacher did not seem to mind; indeed he put in a reference to the mighty power of the Lord which had been shown to Sister Robbins. A chorus of "Glorys" and "Amens" arose, which gave him opportunity to wipe his shining forehead with a red handkerchief.

Presently they sang a hymn, but it was not one of the familiar pretty tunes. They simply chanted over and over again:

> Saved from sin,
> Saved from sin,
> Saved from sin by the Blood of the Lamb.

The fat lady at the harmonium, dominating the chorus by a voice of terrific power, played faster and faster, jerking her turban from side to side as she pumped at the pedals. People swayed or jiggled and clapped their hands. Some of them had tambourines which they rattled to the music. A stoutish man let out a bass howl and moved up the room toward the preacher, bowing his head below his knees at every step.

The harmonium wheezed to a halt at last, and a yellow-faced woman in a stiff hat with long black hatpins began a speech which Minty Lou could not even understand, but it was punctuated by shouts of "Praise the Lord!" and "Hallelujah!" It ended, and the preacher took over, refreshed, until presently he had them singing and dancing again.

Time passed, and the preacher's handkerchief came more and more into play. Perspiration was standing out on other faces, too. Aunt Helen prayed a long prayer. The bosom of the stout lady heaved. Another lady fainted and was tenderly escorted to the storeroom and toilet at the back to recover, but the service went on.

It seemed endless to Minty Lou, sitting and glowering at excitements which were in the first place quite unlike Sunday school and in the second indifferent to what she felt about them. Aunt Helen did not seem to mind whether she joined in, while the other Brothers and Sisters were far too busy themselves to pay her attention. She shut her eyes and tried to pretend she was somewhere else, but she could not do it.

After three long hours, a halt was called. The preacher went over to help the fat lady get up from her bench, while other people fanned themselves or sat down for a moment, frankly exhausted. Presently, however, they all trooped into the back storeroom, each carrying a chair. The preacher took the place of honor in the doorway with the fat lady overflowing a chair by his side. There was a blessing, and everybody began to unpack lunch.

Now Minty Lou could see the reason for Aunt

Helen's generosity with portions. Everyone was
hungry after these exertions and there was a lot to
eat. People commented on the food and swapped
provisions. There was even a good deal left over,
so that Minty Lou not only stuffed herself, but put
a piece of corn bread into her coat pocket. She
felt so much better that she was almost inclined to
think church had been worth it.

Lunch went on for a whole hour. People relaxed
and gossiped and went to the toilet, while a bunch
of the boys and girls escaped from the storeroom
to gather in a group at the edge of the curtain
which concealed the Brothers and Sisters from the
street. One of the boys peeped out. "Raining!" he
said and yawned.

Mellowed by food, Minty Lou made her way
over in their direction with a timid idea of trying
to join the group. One of the girls, a sallow-faced
twelve-year-old, looked at her scornfully. "You the
kid that couldn't hear?"

Minty Lou nodded.

"That couldn't hear nothing?"

"Yeah."

"Not never, you couldn't hear."

"Not since a white lady hit me over the ear with
a ladle," said Minty Lou darkly.

This produced a more sympathetic reaction.
"Got to look out for white folk," one boy remarked. "When they's mean . . ."

"You couldn't hear no sound," the sallow girl interrupted, "until after you come to live with Sister Robbins?"

"That's right."

"I don't believe it," retorted the sallow girl. "What's more, my ma don't either. It's all a trick of that Sister Robbins, Ma says, that's forever setting herself up to be better than other folks is. Why for didn't nobody see you when you was deaf? You didn't come last Sunday, nor yet the Sunday before. You dassn't show youself, that's why."

There was no retort to this but a fight, which was impossible. "I *was* deaf!" insisted Minty Lou in a trembling voice, but she could see the other kids were grinning. "I *was* deaf, so there!" She faced them for a minute, saw it was useless, and walked away, back to Aunt Helen. These people were all unkind, not like Momma said church people ought to be. She hated them.

People were coming out of the storeroom with their chairs to settle themselves again in front of the preacher. Church started over, pretty much the same as before. Minty Lou perceived her enemy sitting by the woman with the stiff back hat and long hairpins. Surprisingly this lady prayed for a blessing on Sister Robbins at the end of a long speech on feeling the Power. Aunt Helen jumped up and prayed back, while the sallow girl

made a face at Minty Lou, who pretended not to
notice. The afternoon wore on until about five
they adjourned to the back room again for cold
tea and the crumbs of the previous feast. Minty
Lou was so stuffed to bursting that she actually
slept through some of the evening session, after
edging her chair up close against the wall. When
she awoke, it was dark outside. Somebody had
opened the door, letting in a cold blast of air. People were gathering bags and baskets, putting on
coats, and shaking hands with the preacher, telling
him that he surely had the Power on this Sunday.
Aunt Helen was in the back getting her things to
go home for supper.

They went back on the streetcar, Minty Lou
standing next to Uncle Elmer and clutching at his
coat when the car jerked. Something about the
weary droop of her mouth stirred him a little, so
that he put an arm around to steady her. Presently
he bent over to say, "You tired after church?"

"It was pretty long," said Minty Lou defensively.

Uncle Elmer hesitated. She was leaning against
his side, a soft, dull weight dragging on his arm.
He had not felt a child so close since he could
remember. He bent down until his mouth almost
tickled her ear. "I think church is much too long,"
he whispered cautiously. "Don't you?"

"I dunno," answered Minty Lou dully. If she

admitted anything, he would surely repeat it to Aunt Helen. Indeed, he might be drawing her out for that very purpose. He was like all the rest.

Uncle Elmer sighed, telling himself it was exactly as Helen said. He ought to leave the kid to her. Besides, if what he had just told her got back to Helen, he'd never hear the last of it.

Josepheen

SCHOOL in that horrible witch dress turned out even worse than Minty Lou had expected. Kids followed her around in recess asking when was Halloween and could she tell fortunes. Minty Lou tried tears and then she tried fighting, but they always thought of something fresh to yell at her.

"Why don't you tie a string around your waist and pull your dress up?" suggested one of the girls after a recess in which Minty Lou had got the worst of a battle. "Them boys might let up beating on you if it was shorter."

This brilliant suggestion made life possible. It was easy to take one of the bits of string which Aunt Helen hoarded and to hitch up her dress the very instant she was out of sight of the house. Neither Aunt Helen nor the school possessed a mirror, so that Minty Lou never quite realized how odd she looked. Luckily her classmates were not really clothes conscious, so that as long as her dress was an average length, they did not often

bother about bloused effects at the waist and irregular hemlines. Minty Lou's high spirits did not
outlast the episode, but the tired teacher and the
easy workbooks afforded some refuge from the
growing difficulties of her outer world.

Minty Lou was gradually plucking up courage
to fight back. Aunt Helen did not shout and had
never laid hands on her since Uncle Elmer had
forbidden it. Although Minty Lou was careful to
do what she was ordered, she could find ways of
showing that she did not like Aunt Helen's household. It was natural, for instance, to quote the au-
thority of school at irritating moments. Practice
soon showed her how far she could safely go, while
no affection or respect restrained her. Aunt Helen
had no experience of this common problem and
was increasingly taken aback. Her only solution
was to keep Minty Lou too busy to play with other
children, since young people naturally liked sin
and encouraged one another. Unhappily, she knew
of no way of preventing her from going to school.
Presently Minty Lou was invited to a birthday
party and made a regular scene when told that
worldly gatherings were sinful.

"All the other kids go," she kept repeating, no
matter how often she was informed that other kids,
brought up in un-Christian ways, were headed for
damnation.

A few days later, untaught by her failure, she
demanded a costume for a school play. She did

not get it, but found some satisfaction in making Aunt Helen angry.

Arguments over this costume dragged on for nearly a week. Scarcely were they over when Minty Lou came home wearing a favor of pink-and-white paper pinned to her dress. Aunt Helen snatched it off and threw it into the garbage.

"But I get to wear it all week," wailed Minty Lou in a tone all too familiar, "because I was best in the class at spelling. Teacher said . . ."

"Don't you *ever* wear such trash!" Aunt Helen shook her.

"It's only for school!"

"You'll not wear ornaments while you live in my house, school or no school."

"But Teacher said . . ."

Aunt Helen, who was used to a quiet home, had come to the end of her patience with these wrangles. Her fingers itched to box Minty Lou's ears, but the child would certainly complain to Elmer. "Go to your room," she snapped, "and stay there." Minty Lou went, abandoning the laundry, which Aunt Helen had to finish by herself.

This kind of thing could not go on. Aunt Helen's efficiency was outraged, her whole way of life upset. When she had undertaken to rear Minty Lou, she had asked no advice from fellow church members with children, thinking of her task as a nuisance rather than a problem. Helen Robbins was a woman who would have been happy in an

exacting professional career. Uneducated, confined
to domestic work, and married to a husband without a tenth of her gifts, she had gone sour. With
age, she had developed a streak of cruelty which
satisfied a thwarted love of power.

Religion was the one piece of color in her life,
and her position among the Sisters was her only
fulfillment. Both were threatened if Minty Lou
could not be molded into a model child. What use
was a miracle if the object of it turned out to be
no good? Aunt Helen felt cheated of a marvelous
experience of power, not by the Lord, of course,
but solely by the willful obstinacy of Minty Lou.

It was not in her nature to give up, though it
had dawned upon her that obedience could only
be enforced by constant battle as long as the girl
had other sets of standards held up to her at school.
Aunt Helen wrung out her clothes and hung them
in the yard, shaking each one viciously as she
struggled in her mind with Minty Lou.

It was necessary to take a firmer stand. She went
up to her attic and fetched down a chamber pot,
a relic from one of her white ladies. She opened
Minty Lou's door and put it inside. Then she
closed the door without a word and locked it.

When Minty Lou did not appear for supper,
Uncle Elmer roused himself to inquire after her.
Aunt Helen told him that the child was naughty
and had been sent to bed. Uncle Elmer shook his
head without comment, but next morning he in-

sisted on Minty Lou's eating a couple of thick
slices of bread spread with drippings from Saturday's roast in addition to her oatmeal.

"She don't deserve it," Aunt Helen protested.

"That's as may be," Uncle Elmer retorted, "but
she can't go fainting in school."

That she might do so had not occurred to Aunt
Helen, but she perceived at once that Elmer had
been right. There was no telling what that girl
might do out of sheer naughtiness. Aunt Helen
had an uneasy fear of getting into trouble which
might disgrace her in the eyes of the Brothers and
Sisters.

It was already spring, and the Brothers and
Sisters used regularly on fine days to take to the
streets. The little harmonium and the fat lady
were lifted onto a donkey cart, which also carried
a box for the preacher to stand on. Everybody
formed into procession and moved off chanting, to
halt eventually in one of the slum streets which
were teeming with people on fine Sunday mornings. The fat lady played the harmonium, while
everybody swung into a hymn or rattled tambourines. The preacher got up on his box and called
the audience to Jesus. Sometimes a few responded
amid shouts of "Glory," and sometimes not. Eventually the donkey went on to another spot, only re-
turning to the church for a late lunch and the
afternoon service.

From Minty Lou's point of view, these outdoor

occasions were worse than sermons inside. She hated being seen with the Brothers and Sisters, especially as the children were sent around with tambourines to ask for pennies. Luckily the church lay well outside her own school district, but she always felt nervous in case a kid in her class might yell out, "Yah! I saw you . . ."

After several weeks, the Brothers and Sisters set up their pitch one Sunday in an alley of broken-down old wooden houses, one of those enclaves of the very poor that still persisted with a single pump downstreet and wooden outhouses tucked away behind in filthy yards. This sort of spot was fruitful soil for a religion which offered drama to drab lives while despising a number of pleasures which no one could afford. A good many joined in the shouting and dancing in response to the preacher's call to come to Jesus. When the children were sent around with their tambourines as usual, a not inconsiderable number of hard-earned pennies was dropped into them or flung down from upper windows.

Minty Lou was doing her part, not willingly, but well enough to escape being blamed, holding her tambourine out as she clambered up shaky wooden steps to push it at people who were staring at the group from their open doors. She never bothered to look at anybody, so that it was without warning that she heard a familiar voice exclaim flatly, "Oh my!"

Minty Lou gave a great start and glanced up.
It was Josepheen, looking dirty in a torn cotton
dress strained over a belly which clearly showed
she had another child coming. Arthureen hung
onto her skirt with one hand, a thumb in her
mouth.

Josepheen and Minty Lou stared at each other.
Even Minty Lou, whose interest in people at this
time was very small, could perceive that Josepheen
had come down in the world. She drooped in the
doorway with one eye swollen half shut where
someone had hit it. Arthureen drooled.

Minty Lou felt quite indignant. Momma had always treated Josepheen like a child who had to be
chivvied and pushed into looking after herself. She
had not done so, which was very wrong of her.

"Oh, Josepheen!" she exclaimed reproachfully.

"Oh my!" said Josepheen again, intent on her
own thought. She never had room for two ideas at
once in her head. "How your ma'd carry on if she
saw you begging for pennies on the open street.
Yes, ma'am, she wouldn't like that!" Josepheen
left her mouth open, forgetting to shut it.

Minty Lou looked at Josepheen and then down
at the tambourine which she was still holding out
with pennies in it. She pressed her lips together
for a minute while she wished that Josepheen
were dead like Momma. How dared she stand
there looking like that and talk about . . . ? "I'm

not begging for pennies," she yelled, losing control. "I don't need them . . . It's only . . . You shut your mouth, Josepheen, and leave me alone!" With a furious gesture, she turned the tambourine upside down so that the pennies bounced on the wooden step at Josepheen's feet. "You take them! You look as if you needed them, so there!" Tears choked her voice as she fled behind the donkey cart.

Aunt Helen had not observed the little scene, but the tall woman with the hatpins was quick to remark that Minty Lou was no longer going about the Lord's business. "Don't never seem to feel the Power neither, not like you'd look for her to, seeing what she claims the Lord done for her hearing. You may do your best, Sister Robbins; but what I always say is, 'Some just don't have a way with them for children.' "

"Don't want for to push her too hard," retorted Aunt Helen tartly. "She still gets the earache bad, for all she has her hearing."

"Ah well, earache's a good excuse for a kid." The tall woman laughed.

Aunt Helen had the sense to make no answer, but she darted furious looks at Minty Lou, who was peering around the corner of the cart at Josepheen. It was a moment when the preacher felt the Power, and the excitement of wrestling for human souls was at its highest. Aunt Helen, angrily keeping Minty Lou in the corner of her eye, was unable to feel the thrill for which she came to church.

She bottled up her wrath till lunchtime, when she could not restrain herself from demanding fiercely what Minty Lou had meant by hanging back.

"I won't beg for pennies in the street," muttered Minty Lou, in her defiant manner. She always got the worst of arguments, but the very struggle had an excitement which had grown irresistible. On this occasion, stirred by an old memory, she added darkly, "I'm not a little monkey in a red jacket."

It was not said particularly loud, but the back storeroom in which they ate their meal was small and crowded. People next her certainly heard, and it was obvious that the remark was going round the circle. Aunt Helen clenched her fist until the nails dug into the palm of her hand. She looked darkly at Elmer, to whom she had said a number of times that a good whipping was the only way to teach the girl her manners. Elmer would not meet her eye. He chewed on his sandwich.

Inwardly Elmer was shocked. He would not have thrashings because he could not bear the thought of them, but he quite agreed that Minty Lou needed a lesson. He did not know what had gone wrong, but he certainly never had imagined that a little girl would speak out rudely in front of everybody. Wasn't she grateful for the trouble people took with her, upsetting their whole lives on her account? Apparently not.

They rode home on the streetcar in a grim silence: Uncle Elmer disapproving, Aunt Helen furious, and Minty Lou frightened. But when they got home, the explosion failed to come. Aunt Helen had had the afternoon to form her plan. "You'll stay in your room by yourself tomorrow," she remarked coldly at bedtime, "and make up your mind to say you're sorry. In future, you'll do exactly as you're told."

Minty Lou looked at her with wide-open eyes of astonishment. "Tomorrow's *school!*"

Aunt Helen's self-control broke down. She seized Minty Lou by the ear, pinching painfully, and hustled her upstairs into her room. She slammed the door and locked it. Uncle Elmer looked up uneasily as she came down. "You really aiming to keep the kid out of school?" he inquired anxiously.

Aunt Helen gave him a piece of her mind. It had taken her the whole afternoon to screw up her courage to the point of defying school. It was well known that school had power to make trouble. Aunt Helen was not sure what could happen, but it was not respectable to get into difficulties with school. All the same, she was intelligent enough

to know that school was her enemy. If she could
have Minty Lou to herself, she would break her in
a week.

"They'll take you down to the jailhouse!" exclaimed Uncle Elmer in panic.

Deep inside, Aunt Helen was frightened; but
she had spirit where Uncle Elmer had none. "I'll
teach that child a lesson," she retorted, "if it's the
last thing I ever do. Don't tell me she don't need
one!"

As Uncle Elmer could not do this, the subject
was closed.

The Restaurant Cook

NOBODY BROUGHT Minty Lou her breakfast next
morning before Uncle Elmer and Aunt Helen
went to work. There would be no lunch. Minty
Lou sat on her bed looking out on the alley, which
was partly concealed by the kitchen roof and a
high back fence. There was not much traffic down
it except the garbage cart or delivery wagons for
the stores on the opposite side. These stores were
all white owned, so that, even had Minty Lou
thought to call for help, she would not have dared.
As it happened, the idea did not occur to her. She
was even careful not to be seen, keeping the lace
curtain between herself and the glass and moving
back into the shadows if anyone seemed to glance
in her direction. Nobody would care that she was
hungry, while Aunt Helen would be angrier than
ever if she called down into the street.

It was one of the first hot days in the year. Sun
blazed in the window. Every so often some white

woman across the way, pausing in her housework, would lean out over the alley, fanning herself. She never stayed long because she had to hurry and help her husband in the store downstairs. On Minty Lou's own side of the alley, which was all colored housing, grownups were out working. Children were with baby-minders or in school.

Minty Lou was used to being rather hungry, but now she was starving. She was thirsty, too. The restaurant cook, coming out in his stained apron, dumped a bursting bag of garbage in his can and spilled a little. A rat slunk into sight to nibble at it. Minty Lou envied him. He vanished like a streak when a black-and-white dog came nosing down the alley. She envied the dog as he finished the mess and moved on. Minty Lou lay back on her bed, too hot to sleep, and thought about food.

When Aunt Helen unlocked her door in time for supper, she was eager to say she was sorry as the price of a meal. Aunt Helen threw a glance of triumph at Uncle Elmer and served her exactly her usual share, no more and no less. "I told you so," she said after a quiet evening. "That taught her a lesson!"

"She was real hungry," pointed out Uncle Elmer uneasily.

Aunt Helen gave an angry sniff. "Now see here, Elmer! There's to be no nonsense about extra food for breakfast. If she has her supper tonight and her oatmeal next morning, she's as fit to go to school as you are to work. Don't you look for to make no more trouble."

In her heart Aunt Helen felt nervous all day lest Minty Lou complain at school or lest inquiries be started over the reason for her absence. As it happened, the tired teacher, who had missed her only because she made no trouble, took it for granted that she had been sick. Children were supposed to come back with written excuses, but a good many of their parents could not write. Teacher made no inquiry and would not have received a truthful answer if she had done so. Minty Lou, like Aunt Helen, was afraid of getting into worse trouble. Besides, she had a terrible weight on her mind. She had stolen a nickel from the box in which Aunt Helen saved small change for church collection and she had bought three doughnuts on the way to school.

Aunt Helen discovered the loss of her nickel that evening. She was too efficient a woman to suppose she had miscounted, and she had little trouble in wringing the truth from Minty Lou, whose conscience told her that people were taken to the jailhouse for stealing. This time she was locked in her room for twenty-four hours, missing supper, together with breakfast and lunch on the following day. She spent a good deal of the time crying, partly from hunger and partly from fear lest a policeman come to take her away. When she was served her usual portion at supper, she put down

her head on the table and howled that she was
hungry.

Uncle Elmer said enough was enough and
forced Aunt Helen to serve Minty Lou as much
as she wanted. But the full meal on an empty
stomach proved too much to digest, so that she
presently retched it away in the bathroom, twisted
in agony by griping pains in her stomach.

Aunt Helen put her to bed and fetched the hot-
water bottle, telling Uncle Elmer that the child
was sickening for something. He had done the
worst possible thing by interfering, and she would
thank him in the future to leave things to her.
Uncle Elmer, horrified by the result of his kind-
ness, promptly agreed.

There could be no doubt that Minty Lou was
ill next morning. Aunt Helen brought up her
breakfast and lunch and left her in bed. She did
not get up all day, or Thursday either. On Friday
when she went back to school, the teacher did not
need to ask if she had been sick. She actually suggested that Minty Lou might want to go home
again, but the child shook her head.

She recovered over the weekend, while Aunt
Helen congratulated herself on victory. The child
went around with her tambourine on Sunday,
looking at Aunt Helen with an imploring appeal
in case she found fault. The lesson had been effec-
tive and, more important still, school had not com-

plained. It had required real daring to take the risk.

"What's the matter with that kid?" asked another teacher quite casually in recess the following Monday. "Didn't she used to be lively?"

The teacher shrugged her drooping shoulders. "Dunno. Been sick, I guess; but she don't say."

Minty Lou was afraid to say, event to her classmates. Grandma had often threatened to send her to the orphanage, while Gordie had filled her full of horrible stories about what happened there. Even Aunt Helen was better than such a fate. She made a desperate resolution to stay out of trouble.

Aunt Helen, after tasting victory, was quite incapable of refraining from using her power. Giving Minty Lou orders to wash or polish after school, she added threats. When the work was not to her satisfaction, she threatened again. Now that the household was quiet as it used to be, she told herself that she had to keep it that way. She could hardly see the child without finding fault because the nervous energy which she usually dammed up inside herself was taking control. Aunt Helen had been a good woman all her days, and it never occurred to her that the line may wear thin which separates one's sanity from madness.

Uncle Elmer made no further effort to help. He knew Minty Lou had been naughty and readily believed what his wife told him. He did not real-

ize that alternate days of starvation and regular
meals amounted to torture. Nor did he notice the
child's appearance, being shortsighted and having
left off attempts to smile at her. It was a relief
that she was quieter, and this could be put down
to Helen's credit.

Two days of the following week Minty Lou
shut up, and for three she went to school. In the
third week since the conflict had begun, she was
shut up on Monday and Tuesday.

She knew the routines of the alley by heart: the
deliveries of candy and newspapers to one store,
hardware to another, meat or a box of Friday fish
to the restaurant. She knew the latchkey kids who
played after school in the alley, putting off the
moment of using the keys strung around their
necks till Ma came home. Between two and three,
when lunch in the restaurant was over, the cook
came out to cram garbage into his dusty can and
slam the lid. It looked messy, but it was food; and
at that hour the alley was generally empty.

Under Minty Lou's window, the kitchen roof
sloped away, smooth and without handhold. She
might sit on it and inch down on her bottom. She
might stop at the gutter perhaps; and if she was
clever, she might swing down from there to the
yard fence. But, having got down, there would
be no possible way to get back up. So what would
happen if the white man caught her rooting in
his garbage? What would happen in any case when

Aunt Helen came home? She quaked with terror at these thoughts, but in that garbage sitting out in the sun there was food. A half-eaten roll lay beside it in the dust.

If she used her sheets for a rope, she might possibly manage to climb up the fence and struggle back onto the roof. In the long distant days, Poppa had taught her to tie square knots. He was good with his hands. Minty Lou ripped off a sheet and tied it by one corner to the bed. Uncertain whether it would reach far enough, she added the other. Jerking cautiously at the knots, she found they held.

She put her head out of the window to look up the alley, which seemed empty. Nobody was leaning out to watch Aunt Helen's roof. Minty Lou took the sheet rope in her arms and climbed onto the windowsill, heart in her mouth.

The roof was steeper than it had looked, and higher, too; but she held onto the sheet and slithered down. A nasty moment came when she had to roll off the gutter, reaching with her feet for the yard fence. Luckily it was a high one and not too far away. When she stood on it, the kitchen roof came down to her chest. It would be possible, if difficult, to wriggle back up.

She tiptoed across the yard and peered through the gate. There was an open door in the restaurant kitchen, which was a lean-to like Aunt Helen's. Through the screen she could hear the sound of dishes clattering as somebody washed up. A fan whirred, gently wafting a rich odor of fried onions which gave Minty Lou a cramp in her empty stomach.

There was no fenced yard to the restaurant, merely a flagstone pavement for deliveries and a storage shed secured by a stout padlock. Minty Lou kept the shed between herself and the kitchen as long as she could. The garbage pails, however, stood right beside the door, so that she had to come out in full sight and cross the pavement.

It took her a while to get up her nerve. There was no sound in the kitchen but the gentle whir of the fan and the washing up. Once she got past the doorway, she could not be seen unless somebody came out.

It was now or never. Pretty soon, the alley would fill up with latchkey kids when school was through. Minty Lou darted across the flagstones, feeling them hot beneath her bare feet in the burning sun. She got to the garbage pails and wrestled gently with the lid of the nearest. It gave with a slight clatter. She stood rooted with fear, but water running in the kitchen seemed to have drowned the noise.

She put the lid on the ground and bent over the garbage. Since the can was never washed and stood in the sunshine, the odor trapped in it was very noisome. The top layer, however, was recent enough to be picked over. Lettuce leaves and bits

of gravy, remains of custard pudding and gobs of
melted fat slipped through her fingers, but there
was a good deal of bread and a big steak bone
with fat and shreds of meat still clinging to it.
Minty Lou picked off pieces of outer onion skin
and gnawed it greedily.

"Hey you there! What you doing?"

Minty Lou had been too absorbed to notice the clattering in the kitchen had stopped. She snatched a piece of roll and was off like a frightened rabbit, two jumps ahead of the cook, who came bursting out of the screen door and pursued her to the edge of his flagstones. Minty Lou leaped across the alley, slammed Aunt Helen's back gate, and bolted it. She rushed for the corner where the fence met the kitchen. She pulled herself up the roof, half sliding, half crawling. Tumbling over the sill onto her bed, she bundled the sheets inside and collapsed panting, awaiting with terror the hue and cry to follow.

"Gott . . . im . . . Himmel!" exclaimed the cook, who had come over from the Old Country as a baby, but who sometimes under stress went back to the language his parents spoke. He turned to his wife, who was peering out of the screen door to see what had happened, raising his shoulders in a helpless shrug and spreading his arms. "You see that, Mary Ann?"

"See what? I was a-setting just a minute over a cup of cold coffee when you yelled. Didn't get my weight off my feet since noon." Mary Ann was a heavy woman with ankles thickened by standing. Her voice was resentful.

"There was this kid." The cook shook his big head from side to side. "A colored brat this high in a long dark nightgown or some such sort of thing. Queerest sight I ever did see, and . . ."

"Them cats have gotten into our garbage again," interrupted his wife sharply. "It's all scattered about. You got to put the lid on real tight, like I told you."

The cook looked at the stinking can. "Not the cats. The kid. That's what I'm telling you, Mary Ann. This kid was eating out of our garbage."

"Not the *garbage,* Ed! You don't mean it!" Even Mary Ann was shocked.

"When I come out, she lit off like an alley cat. Went through thataway and shinnied up that roof there." He pointed. "Had some sort of rope hanging down. Got in through the window."

"You don't say!" Both peered at the window beneath which Minty Lou was crouching.

"What's going on?" demanded the cook. He put his hand to his upper lip and scarped his mustache across his nostrils while he considered. "Eating our garbage! Who lives in that house, for God's sake?"

"How should I know? That whole row's colored. Might as well ask me the names of the alley cats. Might better, and you know it."

"Something ain't right," persisted the cook. "Climbing into a window like somebody locked her upstairs! What's going on?"

"Maybe she's sick," Mary Ann tapped her forehead, "in the head."

"Maybe," allowed the cook doubtfully.

"You never know what goes on with them colored folk," argued Mary Ann. "Besides, you can't afford to get into no trouble, Ed. You're in business."

"But a little kid, Mary Ann," said the cook, appealing to his wife in a manner that made her stiffen up and answer tartly that she didn't go for that soft talk. He made no answer to what was evidently an old argument, merely wiped his hands on his belly apron and sighed. It was a lasting grief to them both that they had only the one daughter, and she married to a butcher in Chicago so that they never got to see their grandchildren. Ed was for adopting all the little kids on the block, which Mary Ann declared was bad for business. Nobody wanted kids crawling around the restaurant tables.

"There! That's a customer come in!" said Mary Ann sharply. "Late lunch most like. You'd best get back to fill the order." She vanished.

The cook scratched his head, glanced once more at Minty Lou's window and, giving up the problem, went indoors.

Minty Lou went to school for the next two days, oppressed by fear lest the white man complain to Aunt Helen. Nothing happened, until on Friday Aunt Helen left her locked up again. She wrestled with temptation, but it was a foregone conclusion that she would lose. Her sheets were ready to throw out on the roof an hour before the cook came out to stuff his garbage into the can. It took him a long time.

Hardly had he turned his back before Minty Lou was out on the roof. She darted across the alley like a shadow and gained the garbage can. The fan was whirring, but there did not seem to be anyone in the kitchen. She lifted the lid. The garbage was neater than the other time. There was actually a piece of newspaper tucked down over it, and on the newspaper lay a package folded carefully between two napkins.

Minty Lou snatched the packet with trembling hands. It contained slices of chicken, a couple of big buttered rolls, and a piece of cake. This might be a trap to catch her stealing a full meal right out of the pail. Minty Lou did not wait to find out, but was off like the wind. It was not easy to climb up the roof with all that food; but she had the string that she tied about her waist, so that she managed. Presently with a piece of chicken in her mouth she was peering through a corner of the lace curtain. Nothing happened and nobody came out. The garbage pails baked in the sun.

Inside the screen door, the cook turned to his wife. "You see, she came for it. I frightened her off for a couple of days, but she came back."

"That's terrible!" Mary Ann's sympathies were aroused by seeing for herself. "Poor skinny little kid!"

The cook pulled nervously at his mustache. "Wednesday afternoon when I dropped down to the store to get tobacco, I went round Myrtle to look at the front of that house. It's number twenty-four."

"See anyone?"

"Nope. Steps whitened and lace curtains in the windows, same like they've got in back. Looks decent enough."

"Ask anyone who lives there?"

"What's the use?"

Mary Ann agreed to this. "The story that you was asking around would've been inside number twenty-four in ten minutes. Then what?"

He nodded, struggling with a conviction which had come to him in the night watches, but which so far he had not ventured to put to his wife. "You know what, Mary Ann," he said. He cleared his throat. "Well, it ain't right what's going on, whatever it is. That poor little kid . . . you know . . . I think it might be a case for the police."

"Police!" Mary Ann stiffened in outrage. "We're in business! You going soft again, Ed? We can't have police come in and out asking questions and making you go to court. Let alone getting in bad with the colored crowd as could easy set a light to your store shed after dark. You crazy, Ed?"

He sighed reluctantly, giving up the notion. "I know, but the kid . . ."

"You mind your own business!" Mary Ann told him sharply. "You're feeding her, ain't you?

That's doing plenty if you ask me. Now leave it alone!"

The cook did leave things alone for a week, during which Minty Lou came down for food every school day but one. Mania was growing on Aunt Helen, who reassured herself because confinement was not making the child seriously ill. No doubt she did not need half what she usually ate. It would be wisest to keep her away from school altogether. There was no trouble from that quarter, and Aunt Helen had convinced herself there never would be.

On Wednesdays after three the restaurant closed, on which occasions the cook would stroll down the street for a packet of tobacco and take a glass or two of beer in the saloon. Naturally he talked to friends and neighbors, who passed the word on in their turn, with the result that quite a number of people down the street watched out for Minty Lou. Nearly all of them shrugged shoulders. As long as the restaurant was feeding the kid, it was none of their business. They weren't neighbors to colored folk. Let those that lived on Myrtle do something about it.

"She's shut up in the back," the cook pointed out.

"Don't tell me the kids next door don't know she's there." It seemed unlikely that they would not, and in point of fact they did. Since, however,

Minty Lou had never come out to play, they did not miss her.

The general impression in the white stores was that the colored had their own ways and no good came of interfering. The man in the cigar store who had five children of his own, took a bit more interest. "Why ain't that kid in school?" he inquired. "She old enough?"

The cook was certain that she was. Minty Lou was tall for her age.

"Why don't the school come around after her, then? They got truant officers . . ."

"You sure . . . in colored school?"

"I guess so," the cigar store owner said. "I'll ask around." He had colored customers.

"Thanks, Bill. You happen to know where the colored school is?"

Bill reflected. "There's one off Pine and one on Wilson . . . maybe a couple of others around. You know how it is."

The cook thanked him for the information. Mary Ann might even buy the idea of a truant officer, though he couldn't quite see himself barging into a colored school and asking about a little girl on 24 Myrtle. What kind of an office would they have there anyway? It wouldn't be easy for him to get off during school hours, what with breakfasts stretching right on into lunch. That kid in and out of the garbage like a skinny little rat! It wasn't right.

Truant Officer

THE SCHOOL TRUANT OFFICER arrived at Aunt Helen's at the tail end of a thunderstorm a few days later. She was a white woman in a well-worn braided skirt and a dark blouse that she was making do for an extra day with a clean collar. "Helen Robbins?" she inquired in her finicking white accent, shaking out her wet umbrella and stepping in to prop it in a corner of Aunt Helen's vestibule. "Mind if I come in?"

There was no question in her tone of voice; and Aunt Helen, still in her working uniform, knew better than to argue with white ladies. She watched the stranger take off her rubbers in silence and led the way into the parlor. She had not happened to work for this sort of white lady, but she knew the type — mousy bun of hair and stiff straw hat set straight on her head like a man's. Recognizing trouble, she gathered her wits. Not even religion suggested that it was any use telling the truth to white ladies, who never understood anything but the answer they wanted. Tight-lipped, she admitted that the little girl that lived with her was Minty Lou Payson, an orphan and seven years old, her own brother's grandchild. Yes, she had had her for three months. No, she was not her nearest relation. "Her own grandma, that couldn't stand her ways no more, give her to me."

This thrust appeared to make no impression. The visitor merely moved in to attack, inquiring directly why Minty Lou was not in school. She was sick? Upstairs in bed? "I'll go and see her if you don't mind." She rose to her feet.

Aunt Helen got up to stand in her way. She was shorter, but broader. Her hand went out to one of the pink vases with gilt edges; her fingers stroked it. In the half darkness of the curtained room, it would have been hard to see if her expression reflected strange impulses. Certainly the visitor did not suspect them. She challenged briskly, "Locked in, eh?"

Aunt Helen started, and the vase fell over. She set it carefully back on its base with a hand that did not tremble. After all, she was a woman of great common sense who had experience in dealing with white ladies. She said easily:

"Yes, ma'am, indeed she is, for her own good. I'm out all day, and there's no telling what she'll be up to when my back is turned. You ask her grandma if she could raise her! She's a bad girl, ma'am, but I took her; and I'll do right by her the best I can."

It was a good speech, but without effect. The visitor looked her firmly in the eye and said sternly, "You'll be lucky if you don't find yourself in court for locking that child up day after day without any food."

Aunt Helen quivered, more with rage than fear, for she was intelligent enough to perceive that the very threat meant that a warrant was unlikely. "You listen to a child that's known for a liar; and then you come to my house and threaten me! That kid has all the food she needs. Now, ma'am, it ain't right to call us names on her say-so. You ask the neighbors whether we ain't God-fearing folk, and decent, too."

The officer sat down again uninvited, placing her feet in their sensible shoes neatly together. "Now, Helen . . ." She did not demean herself to call the colored woman by her lawful married name. "Now, Helen, sit down and tell me calmly all about it."

"Yes, ma'am." Aunt Helen sat, folding her hands upon her lap and assuming the expression which she kept for her white ladies. "I beg your pardon, ma'am, for speaking out, but you'll never know half the trouble I had with that little girl — her grandma too. You can't believe a word she says, and that's a fact."

"She hasn't said anything as far as I know. It's the neighbors that complained."

Aunt Helen was deprived of speech for several seconds. She swayed a little in her chair literally dizzy. It had never occurred to her that Minty Lou would call out of the window, but now she saw how it must have been. If she had caught her, she would have choked the breath out of her. No use thinking of that but she felt savage. Some of the neighbors disliked Aunt Helen because she had found salvation and kept herself to herself. Some envied her because she had lace curtains in her windows and the best parlor on Myrtle Street. There was no end to the malice of jealous neighbors.

"What neighbors?" she demanded hoarsely. Joining with the kid to drag her down!

"They saw her," said the visitor, not condescending to answer. "And I watched her with my own eyes this afternoon. She was climbing out of your upstairs window and going over to the garbage cans in back for something to eat."

"Eating *garbage!*" Aunt Helen raised her hands in genuine horror. "Garbage! There's good cooking in my house and plenty of food. She only done it to make scandal, ma'am — and me wondering why she don't seem to fancy her supper! Believe me, ma'am, she don't need to eat no garbage."

Perhaps if the truant officer had not taken the precaution of lurking in the restaurant kitchen to

watch for herself, she might have been shaken.
The story was a wild one, hardly fitting this
woman in her sober parlormaid costume. As far
as anyone could tell in the semi-darkness of the
stuffy, overfurnished parlor, she was taking the
news as a decent woman might. It was not impossible that the little girl was trying to make
trouble, faking illness at home and loss of appetite,
while pretending to the outside world she was
being starved. Children were naughty in the oddest
ways.

On the other hand, the truant officer had actually
seen Minty Lou, a skinny little bundle of bones
draped in that peculiar garment. The dress in
itself was something odd. She eyed "The Soul's
Refuge" over the mantel. It was too emotional
to go with this stiff room. Grown people were just
as queer as children, sometimes queerer. In any
case, she would have to talk to Minty Lou.

She did not get far in the interview which
followed. Confronted by a stiffly corseted white
lady sitting in the parlor, Minty Lou would only
answer in a scared whisper. Yes, she did like going
to school, and she did like Teacher. No, she didn't
know Teacher had given a very good report about
her schoolwork. She was sorry about taking the
garbage, but she hadn't thought she was doing any
harm. She didn't know whether she was hungry, or
when she had last had a proper meal, or whether
she was happy with Aunt Helen. With the orphan-

age in the back of her mind, she just would not say.

The truant officer sighed inwardly. The child was frightened, that was certain, but of what? Of having been found out? No promise of protection reassured her. What was more, though scared, she looked vicious, for all the world like a little rat cornered. Uncle Elmer, drawn into the questioning when he got home, could only shake his head in horror and, torn between desire to defend his wife and his natural compassion, mutter that Helen knew best, the kid had been naughty, they weren't too used to children, either of them, and who would have thought it.

"She can't stay here," concluded the truant officer. "I daresay you did your best for her, Helen, but it's always hard to manage children when you have had none of your own."

Aunt Helen still held herself well. Her dignity in the world that mattered to her might be lost, but she would not betray the fact to a white lady. "You ask her grandma if she didn't fly at young Gordie and give him a mark he'll carry to his grave. She's a bad girl, ma'am, and the onliest way to deal with her 'd've been to treat her rough. But I never raised a hand to her except the once when she took a fancy she wouldn't go to church. Look her over if you want to, ma'am. There's not a mark on her."

"We have a home for truant children who have gotten out of hand."

"That's where she belongs, ma'am," agreed Aunt Helen with satisfaction.

"But as long as her teacher says she is quiet and attentive and has an excellent school record, I can't get her in. I suppose her grandmother will have to take her back. Would you like that, Minty Lou?"

The question was put without much interest. The problem was how to dispose of Minty Lou, not what she wanted. Even the cook, lurking at the corner of Myrtle to watch the officer go into Aunt Helen's, never gave a thought to what would happen next. Basking in the approval of his conscience, he went home to suggest to Mary Ann that their Annie might be willing to send her oldest girl from Chicago. A week later when the cigar store owner inquired about the kid who was eating his garbage, he had to pause to collect his thoughts. "Oh, that one! I guess the truant officer fixed her. She ain't been back . . . We just heard from our Annie . . ."

Meanwhile, the truant officer, arriving at Grandma's to settle the affair, was received with dismay. Since ridding herself of Minty Lou, Grandma had never inquired after the child for fear that Helen would try to give her back. Until the brat had gone, she had never realized what an irritant her presence had grown to be. Grandma's energies were far more equal to rough and ready housework than to the task of making

Minty Lou do most of it. What was more, now that Minty Lou had gone, Arlene was forced to help.

"I won't have her back, you'd better believe it," she insisted. "I dassn't. Not after what she done to my poor Gordie . . . Gordie! Come here and show the lady what she done."

The officer looked at the mark in silence. Bert, who was in the middle of a quarrel with Gordie about ownership of a battered bicycle they used for delivering papers, remarked sulkily, "It was all Gordie's fault for setting on her with a knife."

Grandma gave Bert a cuff, but the damage was done.

"It's your responsibility," the white lady said in awful tones. "If you don't want her, you will have to find somebody else to take her in. Hasn't the child any other relatives, for instance?"

This speech brought the results which were intended. Grandma, threatened by she knew not what, temporarily lost her head. "There's Sam'l and Ar'minta Hayes in Cambridge as is her grandpa and grandma on Lou's side. Why for shouldn't they take her just as much as me, seeing that it was all the fault of that Lou, as was a bad wife to my poor Jim and killed him."

The truant officer nodded approvingly. She had not needed to follow most of Grandma's speech. The information that there were grandparents in Cambridge down the Bay solved the problem by removing Minty Lou from the Baltimore district, so that no follow-up would ever be required. In her experience, these orphan slum children were never satisfactorily disposed of, so that work on their behalf was fruitless and unending. It would save trouble if the home would take them from the start instead of waiting until they were incorrigible. "These grandparents," she asked, "would be willing to take her?"

Grandma reflected. Neither Aunt Helen nor the truant officer had said a single word about insurance. That little nest egg had been safe for so long that it seemed comfortably her own. The prospect of those Hayeses trying to make a claim was less alarming than it had been at first. "They ain't got much to do with," she concluded, "but they'll take her."

"Well, that's a solution, then." The truant officer closed her notebook, put away her pencil, and rose to her feet. "You'd better put her on the boat, and buy her a ticket. The stewardess can look after her, I daresay, and set her off in Cambridge. How soon can you arrange it?"

"Saturday's my half day. I'll put her on the *Joppa* and she'll be in Cambridge Sunday morning, ma'am."

"You mean tomorrow?" The truant officer, who had already taken a few steps toward the door, paused, puzzled. "How can you let them know or get an answer saying that they'll have her?"

"I was forgetting the day," said Grandma hastily, perceiving that in her anxiety to get rid of Minty Lou she had nearly overreached herself. She had no idea how to send word to the Hayeses, who did not after all know that Lou was dead. There was some feller working on the *Joppa,* but she didn't rightly recall. Besides, the Hayeses might refuse if they were asked. It would be better to let them sort everything out for themselves — take their minds off the insurance. Once Minty Lou was actually on their doorstep, they could not easily ship her back. "Tomorrow week's the day. I'll fetch her from Helen, who'll see her clothes is packed. That suit you, ma'am?"

It suited the truant officer so well that she took her leave briskly and strode off in the glow of a good conscience. It was not often that she came up with a satisfactory answer to a problem of this kind. A fresh start in Cambridge . . . a new set of faces. She could not imagine that it would do much good for that little rat; but if she worried over things which could not be helped, her job would kill her.

The Voyage

AFTER THE VISIT of the truant officer, Aunt Helen refused to speak an unnecessary word. On Sunday, she left Minty Lou at home with housework while she and Uncle Elmer went grimly off to church to face inquiries. At the end of the week, she handed over a small, basketwork suitcase with a broken catch and an elderly strap to go around it, instructing her to pack her clothes because Grandma was coming to put her on the Saturday boat for Cambridge, where she was going to live with her Grandpa Hayes.

Minty Lou spent Saturday morning washing out her sheets and removing her blankets to a storage chest in the attic. Uncle Elmer took down her little iron bed and set up a wooden one with a shiny brown headboard. Aunt Helen ironed a cotton damask spread for it. There was nothing left to show that Minty Lou had lived there, except the suitcase with her old winter coat draped across it, and one of the witch dresses hanging in the wardrobe, clean and ironed, all ready to put on.

Grandma arrived after lunch carrying a sandwich and an apple in a paper bag. "That's your
supper," she said, handing it to Minty Lou. "You
won't need no breakfast, seeing as how *Joppa* gets
in to Cambridge wharf round six o'clock." She
looked about her, admiring Aunt Helen's parlor.
"Tain't fancy with them Hayeses, not like the
beautiful home that you've had here. You better
aim to make the best of it because you ain't
a-coming back no more to me."

Minty Lou nodded silently without looking up.
There'd be beans most days in Cambridge with
a bit of pork on Sundays. Grandpa would send
her out to work and keep her money. There'd be
older kids to bully her, and she'd sleep on the
floor. But she was frightened by her narrow escape
from the delinquent home, and she had to live
somewhere.

Grandma would have dearly loved to give the
sulky brat one of her good cuffs, but she, too, had
been scared by the white lady from school. She
said tartly, "Well, what you standing around for?
Get your things and say good-by to your aunt.
Mind you thank her for all she done.

"She's out," muttered Minty Lou. Aunt Helen,
efficient to the end, had avoided good-bys.

Grandma picked up the little suitcase, while
Minty Lou followed with the coat and sandwich.
Grandma grumbled at the streetcar fares on the

way over, and she rummaged a long time in her
bag for seventy-five cents for the steamboat ticket.
"Had to pawn your ma's glass bowl," she announced in farewell, "to get that dollar. I give
that stewardess a quarter of it to look after you
and put you off in Cambridge. I done my duty
by you. Now let your ma's folks have you for a
change." Still muttering, she made her way back to
the streetcar stop, a load off her mind.

The *Joppa* was an elderly side-wheeler which
made the Choptank River run three times a week.
She carried a mixed cargo of freight and passengers
which she dumped off at little country wharves
down the eastern shore of the Chesapeake Bay and
up the Choptank. In return she took on crabs kept
fresh in layers of seaweed, barrels of oysters, eels
pickled in brine, fresh eggs, calves for the slaugh-
terhouses, fruit and vegetables in season, white
men on business, and colored folk drifting up to
the big city looking for work. The stewardess, who
was a neat little woman with a harried expression,
took Minty Lou into the saloon and settled her on
a wooden bench, telling her not to move on any
account. She trotted away at a gait between a walk
and a run, leaving Minty Lou by herself.

Second-class passengers were mostly out on the
stern deck watching the cargo come aboard or
saying good-bys. Minty Lou had the colored end
of the saloon to herself — dark brown and dingy
with dirty windowpanes and scuffed wooden

benches. Across a gangway lay the first-class section, dark brown and gilt with big mirrors and
faded red plush chairs. Around a counter at the
far end stood a group of white men drinking beer.
Minty Lou sat still as a mouse, hoping not to be

noticed. She had never so much as been on a street-car alone.

The cargo came aboard with a great deal of shouting, thundering sounds of iron wheels, and creaking of winches. A couple of stout ladies with bulging string bags bustled into the colored section to fuss about choosing seats. They stared at Minty Lou, and one of them said something to the other; but luckily they did not try to speak. Minty Lou wondered whether they would object if she ate her apple. Presently she did so, taking small furtive bites and holding it down in her lap to conceal what she was doing.

The stewardess trotted into view with a pile of linen, pausing by Minty Lou to say, "You stay right there!"

"Can't I help you make beds?" offered Minty Lou timidly, eager for protection from the strangers in the saloon.

The stewardess shrugged tired shoulders. "All right, but don't leave the suitcase if you want to see it again." She whisked off, leaving Minty Lou to stumble after.

They put her suitcase in a smelly little cabin without ventilation except for a grille in the door. "You don't want to sleep in the common bunk-room," the stewardess said, "not a little kid like you, believe me! There ain't but the one bunk here, but you can double up with me." She locked the

door and led the way to the top deck, moving
faster than ever to make up for lost time.

Minty Lou was still making up the first-class
cabins when the *Joppa* cast off and inched out into
the bay amid a series of long toots. When she came
out of one cabin to go into another, the water was
sliding past at a terrifying speed, churned into two
great wakes by the *Joppa*'s thrashing paddles.
Baltimore harbor had dwindled into a confused
mass of wharves and shipping concealing behind
it every place familiar to her. She had no regrets,
but deep down she was frightened and would, if
the chance had been given her now, have gone
back to Grandma.

As the sun was setting, the stewardess took
Minty Lou back to the saloon and found her
a seat on another bench next an elderly lady
who had gone to sleep with her head against the
wall. "Now you set down right there and don't
you talk to no one. Eat your supper, and I'll fix
up the bed when I get time." She produced a
muddy cup of lukewarm coffee for Minty Lou
and scampered off.

Both halves of the saloon were crowded, and
spittoons were in constant use. The atmosphere
was cloudy with tobacco smoke and flavored with
a rich mixture of fish, beer, and whisky. In the
plush and gilt section, people were sitting around
tables, while waiters in white coats moved among

them. Colored passengers had unpacked sandwiches or liquid refreshment. Minty Lou noticed
that many did not eat what they had by them.
She would have liked to ask for some, being still
hungry; but the stewardess had told her not to
speak. Besides, they were a noisy crowd, mostly
young men. In one corner there was a crap game
going. The elderly lady sitting next Minty Lou
did come to life and start conversation by asking
where she was getting off; but Minty Lou, too
timid to answer, pretended she had not heard. The
lady gave a disapproving sniff and went back to
sleep.

Long after it was black outside, the stewardess
returned to take her to the cabin, which was now
lit by a smelly lamp in a bracket. "We ain't
allowed sheets," the stewardess said, "except the
used ones; but I saved us a good pair."

There was nowhere to wash, not even a basin
in the toilet. Minty Lou took her dress off and
hung it on a hook. She put her shoes under the
bunk, and the stewardess tucked her in tight
because it was narrow and there had to be room
for them both, one head at each end. She blew
out the light and went away, shutting the door.

She came back a long time later and found
Minty Lou restless. "You not asleep yet?"

"The chinches is biting," protested Minty Lou.
She had met bedbugs at Grandma's, but not by
the million.

The stewardess made a clucking sound of annoyance, but she fetched a can of powder which she scattered all up and down the blankets, over the mattress, and into cracks in the bulkhead. She climbed into bed at last, fitting herself so tightly against Minty Lou that neither of them could well turn over. "Now go to sleep."

Minty Lou did doze off, either because the powder had helped with the chinches, or because she was just too tired to stay awake. In either case, she seemed to have slept about five minutes when she was awakened by the most tremendous clatter, accompanied by shouts and thumping at the partition against which her body was crammed. She sat up in panic, wondering if the *Joppa* was sinking.

"Go to sleep!" The stewardess kicked her down indignantly. "They're coming into Tilghman's, getting cargo ready to put out on the wharf." Judging by the noise, Tilghman's was receiving a consignment of freight cars which had been stowed behind the rest of the cargo. The bulkhead of the cabin was only plank through which one could see cracks of light from the lanterns which the porters had lit up to sort things out.

Eventually Tilghman's received its goods. The gangway was drawn in again with a final rumble. Lights were extinguished, and the throb and thrash of the paddle wheels resumed their rhythm. Tilghman's lay at the head of the five-mile estuary

formed by the Choptank River as it joined the
Chesapeake Bay. The *Joppa* moved majestically
upstream through the night, pitching less as the
rollers of the great bay gave place to smaller
waves. Once more, Minty Lou dozed.

It took about an hour from Tilghman's up to
Bellevue, where the whole performance of noise
was repeated again, merging imperceptibly into
that of Oxford, ten minutes' farther on. Minty
Lou tried to lie still and not fidget, but she could
not. The stewardess, who was used to sleeping
through noise, complained.

Luckily about two in the morning the *Joppa*
crossed the Choptank River, zigzagging back to
go up its southern side. This maneuver took an
hour and a half, during which time peace reigned
in the cabin. After that, the noise started up again,
as loud as before.

"Why don't you let me go out, ma'am?" asked
Minty Lou at four o'clock as preparations for yet
another landing got under way. "I won't be no
trouble, ma'am — just stand and watch. I can't
sleep no more."

The stewardess gave way. Her conscience told
her that she ought to keep Minty Lou beside her,
but reason insisted she had to have her sleep before
she faced another day. "You go straight back to
the saloon when they pulls in the gangway. No
hanging about in the dark with those rough men.
They's always people that sleeps in the saloon, and

it'll be quiet by now. You're all right there." Minty
Lou got dressed, put on her coat and her shoes and
tiptoed out.

There was a mist on the water through which
a lantern was shining dimly from a little wharf,
no more than a shed on a platform set out in the
river at the end of a long plankway built on pilings
which stretched behind it into blackness. No shore
was in sight. The *Joppa* was nosing cautiously in,
its paddle wheels churning, stopping, backing, and
churning again. Two men were standing by to
cast ropes around the bollards which were gleam-
ing wetly in the lantern light. There was an old
man on the wharf, sitting on a pile of crabpots
with the air of one who will not move until the
last moment.

"You got them cartwheels?" he shouted to two
men standing by the gangway ready to slide it
out as the *Joppa* came alongside. "Mr. Michaels
looked for them to come last trip. He was right put
out."

"You got them cartwheels, Joe?"

"Two five-foot cartwheels, one plowshare, ten
empty barr'ls, two pair of oarlocks and a two-inch
rope."

"No paint?"

"No, sir. No paint."

The old man spat into the narrowing water
between himself and *Joppa*. "You ain't never
got a whole order to rights," he grumbled. "Mr.

Michaels he'll be down afore noon and right put
out. It ain't my blame, but Mr. Michaels won't
fancy driving back again two mile to pick up
paint."

The gangway roared out, and the porters began
to trundle empty barrels down it, while the old
man hitched himself up to unlock his shed, where
the rope and the plowshare and the cartwheels
could be stored until they were called for. There
was no cargo to put on, since fish and farm produce were taken up on the return trip. In a few
moments, the *Joppa* was thudding out into the
stream, while the little lantern dwindled into a
pinpoint and vanished. Nothing was visible but
water and mist. It was like traveling from nowhere
into nothing. Minty Lou shivered as she made
for the saloon, where lingering wreaths of stale
tobacco smoke gave a dead look to people sprawled
over the benches amid a scatter of rubbish.

Around five o'clock the first-class passengers for
Cambridge started drifting into the saloon for coffee. People on the benches came to life, rubbing
sore joints. Some unpacked sandwiches, and others
took refreshment out of a bottle. One or two
stumbled out on deck, leaving a door open. A
chilly little breeze wandered in, doing its best
with the stale smells of the saloon.

The stewardess trotted in with Minty Lou's
suitcase. "You all right, kid? She docks in fifteen
minutes."

"Is Cambridge outside?" asked Minty Lou timidly. "Can I go out to look at it?"

"Ain't much to see for mist. It's all flat here, both sides of the river, that's more than two mile wide right up to Cambridge. Who's meeting you, honey?"

It occurred to Minty Lou with a shock that she did not know. There was that old tale about how Grandma Minty had ridden in a jitney down to the wharf to talk to Mr. Prince's brother. Grandpa must live a good way off. Besides, if he came himself, how should she know him? What would happen if she was carried away by the wrong person? She said in a scared voice, "I–I think my grandpa. He's called Mr. Hayes. Do you know him, ma'am?"

The stewardess laughed. "I ain't no country girl, honey. I'll put you out on the wharf, see? And if your grandpa ain't a-waiting, don't you stir, not till he comes. You understand?"

Minty Lou nodded.

Cambridge Wharf

CAMBRIDGE was nothing special to see on a misty morning. The *Joppa* drew up to a wharf with a long wharfhouse, bordered on one side by oystering sheds and lines of shacks for the colored shuckers, who came from as far as fifty miles for oyster season. Upriver, the view was cut off by a big old-fashioned rooming house set in trees and approached by a broad path of oystershells skirting a stable.

A good many passengers who were getting off had brought freight with them, mostly farming gear or supplies for local stores. On the landward side of the wharf, carriages, farm carts, and small horse vans stood waiting, their colored drivers muffled in sacks against the damp air. More freight was being dumped into the storage shed, on the door of which the wharfkeeper was chalking a tally.

Minty Lou put down her suitcase while she looked around her. A porter promptly wheeled

his trolley past it, shaving it with his load as she
skipped aside. The movement brought her in con-
tact with a white man, who pushed her roughly
away as she begged pardon. Nervously she took
refuge beside a pile of boxes waiting to be trans-
ported further upriver.

The stewardess, after putting her on the gangway, had bustled off in hope of tips. Colored
people in sight were either moving freight or
waiting by their horses. The elderly lady who had
tried to speak to Minty Lou last evening plodded
away into town. Minty Lou had an impulse to
run after her and ask about the Hayeses, but after
having once been rude to her, she did not dare.
She crept around to the shore side of the wharfhouse, gaining an indistinct view of a straight
street with the carts in the foreground and the
little old lady trudging off into the mist.

The *Joppa* finished its loading, pulled in its
gangway, and moved on upriver with a farewell
toot. The stewardess did not reappear on deck
to wave to Minty Lou. She had forgotten her
completely in the press of duties. Meanwhile on
the wharf, boxes and barrels were soon sorted out.
Drivers whipped up their animals and rolled off.
The wharfkeeper lingered for twenty minutes,
fussing inside his shed. He went home to breakfast,
hardly glancing at Minty Lou, who was sitting on
her suitcase underneath the little back window
of the wharfhouse. The sun came up, bathing the

white street in a golden haze. It was going to be hot.

Minty Lou went on sitting on the basketwork suitcase, a forlorn little figure with the shabby coat over her lap. The bell of a church clock struck seven. Because it was Sunday morning, no one was stirring early. Soon she moved around into the shade, where a tangle of crabpots and an old boat protected her from being seen.

The clock struck eight. An empty barrow pushed by a colored man came down the street, raising a little cloud of dust which showed how fast the dew had dried. Minty Lou thought of calling out, but she was relieved when he turned off into an alley. She stared at the Choptank River, a color between brown and blue, stirred into faint ripples. The opposite shore was a flat line two miles off with a single white house looking over the water.

Between nine and ten a couple of white boys came out of a big house, while a woman opened a window to tell them to shut the wicket gate of their front yard. Other distant voices suggested that people were moving; and soon after ten, whole families came out of their front doors dressed up for church. They turned their backs on Minty Lou, proceeding in the general direction of the clock, which was concealed from her gaze by chestnut trees.

Minty Lou was hungry and thirsty and beginning to feel unpleasantly hot. She shifted further

into the shade, draping her coat carefully over
the edge of the boat. She wondered when anyone
would come whom she could dare ask about
Grandpa. Maybe he had not appeared because
he did not want her.

Around noon, a working crab boat drifted in
to the wharf, propelled by the gentle breeze. The
men in it looked rough, and they were white.
Minty Lou retreated out of sight, peering occa-
sionally around the shed to watch them landing
bushel baskets of crabs packed in layers of wet
weed. They were grumbling about the weather,
the crabbing, and the state of the tide.

"Crabs will do all right in this here shade,"
one said, "just as long as *Joppa* ain't late. The sun
gets around this far soon after three."

"*Joppa*'s always late on the return run."

"Not on Sundays she ain't when the canneries
ain't working."

"Ah."

The men piled back into their boat and drifted
off downstream. Minty Lou peered after them,
wondering if the stewardess on *Joppa* would take
her back on the return run. Whatever would
Grandma say, and could she actually travel to
Baltimore without a ticket? She had nothing with
her to eat. She sat down by the crab baskets, out
of which a few wiggling claws were poking their
way through cracks. She eyed them hungrily.

Crabs ought to be cooked, but she did not feel

like being fussy. Surely nobody would miss a claw
or two. She examined the nearest, viciously pinching at the air. As she put out her hand, it seemed
to grab for her finger as though it had eyes in it.
She jumped away.

After a minute, she tried again, approaching her
fingers from what seemed the backward side. Eventually she got a grip on the thing and wrenched
it loose. She put the end into her mouth, chewing
on it and spitting out pieces of shell. It tasted
fishy and there was not much inside, but it was
food.

The wharfkeeper returned about two, in plenty
of time for receiving consignments or straightening
out the chalk marks on his door. This being Sunday, he did not expect a rush of produce from the
country, though one never knew, since peas were
getting ripe. Presently he walked around to look
at the crabs, while Minty Lou, still picking at an
occasional claw, dodged quickly away.

The wharfkeeper had a vague idea that a kid
had been hanging around his shed since morning,
but he did not much mind because it had been
locked. He opened it and went inside, coming out
after ten minutes to count the baskets of crab. The
kid was still there. He did not tell her to go home
because it was most likely that she was locked out
of doors while her mother cooked Sunday dinner
for some family in town.

It was not until he noticed the basket suitcase

tucked half under the old boat with the little coat
folded on top that it occurred to him this kid
must have come off the *Joppa*. He looked around
for her, then, but she had dodged out of sight. It
was a mighty queer business. He went back to his
shed to wait until he heard a little scuffle. Popping
round the corner, he caught Minty Lou with a
claw in her mouth.

They stared at one another for a moment, each
paralyzed by a different sort of shock. The wharfkeeper recovered himself first. "You hungry as
that?"

"Oh no, sir! No, sir!" Minty Lou was in a panic.
"N–not anymore!" She looked at the claw in her
hand and wanted to throw it away, but did not
dare to. She was so full of raw crab that she felt
sick. "I didn't mean any harm, sir." She dropped
him a curtsy.

"You come off the *Joppa* this morning?"

"Yes, sir." She put her hand behind her back
to drop the crab claw.

He shook his head from side to side slowly.
Eight hours on his wharf and eating raw crab!
This surely was a new one to him! "You got folks
in Cambridge?"

He almost expected that she had not, that someone had dumped her off on his wharf and gone
away. These colored folk — what they did to one
another! Not like people one knew! It was a relief
to hear that she did have relatives in town, though

he did not know the Hayeses. Couldn't expect him
to remember the fancy names they picked out for
themselves, taken from their old masters most
often. There was a Hayes in town running the
hardware who might know them.

"You wait here a bit," he decided, thinking
things over. "There'll be a couple of head of colored fellows coming down with jitneys to meet the
Joppa. I'll ask around."

"Yes, sir," agreed Minty Lou, her heart beating
madly at the thought of what he would do to pun-
ish her for eating his crabs. She edged away from
him as far as she dared.

The wharfkeeper held in a general way that the
colored should be kept in their place, but it so
happened that he had a grandson who was about
Minty Lou's size and the apple of his eye. Kids
were kids. This one was frightened of him to the
point of running off to hide — and then what?
Skinny little creature! Might have been given a
bad time somewhere, he wouldn't wonder. These
colored folk and their ways!

He surprised himself by saying, "Now you just
come into my shed and set down comfortable.
You're a parcel, see that ain't been called for; so
that it's my job to get you delivered." She looked
about her wildly, but he moved to pen her in so
that she could not dodge him.

"Yes, sir!" she said in trembling appeal as he
grabbed her.

There was not nearly the same amount of bustle on the wharf for the *Joppa*'s return trip. A couple of farm carts came in with early peas, and a good many people who were going up to Baltimore on business came down on foot, by carriage, or by jitney. Most of the jitneys were carts with seats mounted in them, equally handy for passengers or freight, both shaded by a leaky awning on top. These were the property of colored owners who drove a depressing bunch of half-blind bony horses. The driver of one of these jitneys admitted to knowing the Hayeses and having a notion where they lived. He was a little man in a ragged pair of overalls, his face distended by a plug of tobacco. He spat politely into the Choptank and offered to take the kid along. If he remembered right, it was a good way. It involved the sacrifice of a possible fare on the return journey; but Minty Lou did not know this and the wharfkeeper did not care. He filed Minty Lou away in his mind as a good story to tell over a glass in the saloon. It did not occur to him to ask the jitney man next day whether she was all right.

Minty Lou climbed into the cart, and the basket suitcase was stowed under the back bench. The driver said, "Giddy-up!" and jerked the reins. The horse blew sadly and started a decrepit walk, which seemed to be all he could manage. They plodded up the straight street, flanked by pleasant white houses standing in grounds of their own, and began to catch glimpses of a courthouse, a couple of churches, a cross street with corner stores, and more buildings beyond.

The driver was conversational. "You must be Lou's kid, come down on a visit maybe." He stole a glance at her. "You got a look of Lou, but she weren't never skinny. I used to dance with Lou at the old Palace, that caught fire and burned down. Lou was a great one for dancing."

He did not seem to want any answer. Sometimes Minty Lou still dreamed of Poppa and Momma dancing up the pavement like a pair of mechanical dolls twisting to the music, while Freddy Lane's mother and Mr. Prince, and Josepheen and others followed after. The sad-eyed monkey watched them from the cart, or sometimes Minty Lou watched, as they grew far away and small. It was the only dream she ever had about Poppa and Momma, and she always woke up crying because the music made her sad. She felt a prickle in her eyes now, but she blinked it back. It never paid to be soft and you had to be wary of strangers.

The driver was telling her all about the old Palace, where there used to be a couple of kids that had banjos and one that played the drum. On Saturday nights folk walked or hitched a ride from five to ten mile around for the dancing there. "That's how your pa, that was a country fellow, first got to meet your ma. Your ma had big ideas when they went off to Baltimore, and I guess they

done right good." He shook his head. "Maybe
there was too many jitneys in Cambridge like she
said, but I done get this cart when uncle died, and
I got folks in town." He sighed. "Your pa, he
didn't mind going off with her, not like I did."
He flapped his reins on the sad horse and stopped
talking a moment, though the lump on his jaw
moved up and down as though he was still arguing
with Lou.

They were passing straight through the town,
which was not a large one, going through clusters
of smaller houses with early roses just coming out
in their yards and kids tumbling about. "That's
colored town out there." The driver pointed at a
red brick church which reared itself ahead. "Be-
gins around Bethel."

Colored town was a straggling collection of
squatter shacks or rows of identical mean houses
put up by some white tradesman who had invested
his nest egg in colored rentals. It was dusty and
rubbish strewn, with irregular tracks running
through it worn down by feet and ending as often
as not in a slimy puddle where someone had
thrown washing water out on the ground. Except
for the fact that there were open spaces, it was
worse than the row of hovels where Minty Lou
had last seen Josepheen. "I won't stay here," she
said to herself. "Not longer than I have to. As
soon as I'm old enough, I'll get out." She put her
hand to her dress. Momma's badge was still un-

derneath it. Momma hadn't liked Cambridge at all, and she wouldn't either.

They crossed a properly made road which seemed to go somewhere, and the jitney driver pointed out where he lived in a row of wooden houses with horrid little porches on which people sat rocking while children played outside in the dust. "Ain't ten year old," he said with pride, "but believe me, the rent's high!" He sighed. The little houses showed peeling remains of paint and had in general the look of places which were filled to bursting and had already begun to split at the seams. They drove on.

"Sam'l Hayes lives out on the edge o' town," he said apologetically. "Keeps himself to himself — don't buy on the tick nor hang around the store. Works hedging and ditching when the weather's right, and digs a grave when he can get to. Track here's bumpy, because no one don't never drive down it, only the man that comes for the rent."

Minty Lou looked frowningly at an old, green-painted house, just big enough for one room upstairs and one down, with a lean-to kitchen added. There was a well on the near side with a fence around it and a rope on a bucket for drawing up water. Somebody was chopping wood with an ax in the back yard. "That'll be Sam'l," the jitney driver said. "He'll be chopping the week's wood for the stove if I know Sam'l."

The rattle of the old cart was evidently a strange

sound. A girl popped her head out of an upstairs
window, then drew it back in. A moment later she
appeared around the front of the house, mouth
gaping. She might have been about ten, but small
for her age. Minty Lou stared resentfully at her.
"Your dad in?" called the driver of the jitney.

The man with the ax came from behind the
house to join his daughter. He was a big man with
a wide ugly mouth and splayed nose which looked
like Momma's. "Hiya, Frank," he said. "What
you got? That your kid with you?"

"Lou's kid," retorted Frank. "She was a-setting
on the wharf all day with no one come to fetch her.
You forget her, Sam'l, or what? Come down on
the *Joppa* this morning and there wasn't no one
there for her. What's wrong?"

Minty Lou and her grandfather stared at one
another, she wary and unfriendly, and he blank.

"She has a look of Lou," he conceded slowly.
"Where's her ma?"

The jitney driver handed down the basket suitcase and gave Minty Lou the coat to hold. "Mind
out for the step," he said, as he helped her down.

"Ain't heard from Lou," continued the big man,
still puzzled, "not since Ar'minta come back from
Baltimore. That feller Lou knowed that worked
on the *Joppa,* he drifted off. I did ask after him,
but no one knew nothing. So what's going on?"

Minty Lou was not listening; she had too much
to take in. This was the place she was going to live,

with that girl and that big man, who was no more glad to see her than she to see him. Samuel Hayes in his work overalls looked very different from Poppa in his neat pinstripe with the bird on his blue tie. It was rather terrifying to think of being trapped in that little house with that big man. She looked appealingly at Frank, the jitney driver, who was preparing to leave.

"Always had a soft spot for Lou," Frank said, "and maybe if she hadn't gone off to Baltimore . . . but she done good." His eye fell on Minty Lou, and he appeared for the first time to take in the witch dress hitched up with string, the basket suitcase, and the battered winter coat. "That is . . . people used to say . . ." his voice died off.

"Ar'minta!" called the big man, his voice booming out of his great chest as though a shout were natural to his size. "Come out and see who's here, Ar'minta, quick!"

Grandma came bustling out, her smallness making the hugeness of Grandpa Hayes more appalling than ever. She stared at Minty Lou without knowing her for a minute. "That dress, and you so thin!" she cried, recognizing her at last. "Where's my big Lou?"

Minty Lou did hear that, but she thought that Grandma was pretending, just to cover up from Frank why they had not met her. She said resentfully, "Momma and Poppa died ever so long ago, and you didn't come up to the funeral neither."

Her Own Place

GRANDMA MINTY kissed and cried over her, just the way that Grandma Payson had done. It meant nothing, and Minty Lou did not want to cry. Those deaths were too long ago for tears. It was more important that people had not been really glad to see her, only surprised and sorry. She did not tell them much of what had happened to her, merely that she had gone to Grandma's until Grandma would not keep her because she fought with Gordie. So the lady had said to put her on the boat for Cambridge.

"What lady?"

Minty Lou did not say. Grandma had told her never to come back no more, and she had waited a long time on the wharf because nobody came.

"But your clothes!" wailed Grandma Minty. "Lou used to dress you right pretty. Whatever come over Ellen Payson? And you so thin!"

Tears did come to Minty Lou's eyes at that.

"Aunt Helen made all my dresses this way, so that I put the string around to tuck them up."

"Aunt Helen?" Nobody, it seemed, had heard of Aunt Helen; but Minty Lou found she could not talk about her. There was a choke in her throat as tears came pouring down her cheeks.

"Let her be, Ar'minta," Grandpa said in his loud rumble. "She'll tell us in her own time or not at all."

Grandma patted Minty Lou until she stopped crying. Still no one had said anything about being glad she had come. The sitting room was ugly, with nothing in it that was not chipped or split or broken from hard wear. The lino on the floor was worn into holes.

A big boy about as old as Tom came in who was Momma's brother, Mike. The girl was called Marybelle and was the youngest. Neither of them looked glad to see Minty Lou, only surprised. Marybelle asked, "Ma, wherever can she sleep?"

Grandma Minty hesitated. "We'll fix something . . ."

"You can sleep with your ma tonight, Marybelle," Grandpa said. "And I'll make do down here. Tomorrow I'll see if your Uncle Jim still has that bed."

Grandma Minty sighed. "He hasn't."

"Then I'll go on down here for the time being."

Nobody said anything to this. They were not going to let Minty Lou sleep on the floor, but it was not convenient to have her in the house. Grandma took Minty Lou upstairs and showed her which was Marybelle's bed. There was a row of pegs in the wall above it for dresses which were draped over with an old sheet. There were boxes from the grocery store under the bed for underwear. Grandma told Marybelle to settle her in. "And you can take the scissors out of my sewing box to cut the bottoms of them dresses off. I'll hem one up this evening, but I got to get back to cooking the supper." She gave Minty Lou a little kiss and vanished. Things felt better, and presently Grandma's voice was rolling richly from the kitchen.

> Nobody knows de trouble I seen,
> Nobody knows but Jesus.

"Ma always sings that song when she got troubles," Marybelle remarked. "I expect in the city you don't hear them old tunes."

"Not much."

"Ma said you done have a party with a phonograph and all, one of them with a picture of a little old dog a-listening to the music, just like I seen down to the store. I wished I could go to the city." Marybelle was actually looking at Minty Lou with admiring eyes, which was the first time that any such thing had happened since she used to tell tall tales to Josepheen.

"I'm going back as soon as I can," Minty Lou confided. "I don't like it here."

"It's dull in Cambridge," Marybelle agreed.

Supper was ready a bit late, and Minty Lou was hungry again. Grandma's kitchen was hot and stuffy from the wood stove. It was crowded with a couple of flour barrels, a rickety table with a basin for washing up and a tall cabinet with dishes in it. There was a big pot of stew with salt pork mixed with early greens from the garden and potatoes in a thick gravy. There was corn bread, too, big chunks of it fresh and hot. Minty Lou's eyes opened wide, and even after the blessing she did not start to eat.

"You not hungry, honey?" Grandma Minty sounded upset.

Minty Lou smiled her first smile, not at Grandma, but at her own heaped plate. "Oh yes, I'm starved; but first let me just look at all that food!"

She was ready for bed right after supper. It had been a long journey and she was really full. She climbed into Marybelle's bed and fell asleep, never hearing the other two kids come upstairs later on. She woke in the dark, seeing a light reflected up the stairs which rose directly from the living room into the bedroom occupying the whole top of the house. She could hear the rumble of Grandpa's voice and the murmur of Grandma's. Cautiously she stole to the top of the stairs and sat on them to listen because it always paid to know the worst. Sure enough they were talking her over.

". . . dunno how you're to manage," Grandpa was saying. "It ain't so much the food as the cash money for clothes and such. You seen what she was wearing."

"She'll help along with the others and earn a little."

Minty Lou nodded to herself in the dark. Grandma was already planning to put her out to work and keep her wages.

"Never can get no work regular in winter, and there ain't so many eggs to take to the store for cash money. I won't never buy on the tick."

"The Lord will help us, Sam'l," Grandma said. "Ain't He always done it?"

Minty Lou frowned. People talked about religion when they wanted to do something unkind. She didn't trust anyone.

"It ain't what Lou would want for her," Araminta said sighing. "I can't help but think of that — so proud she was of her big job and the ideas she had for Minty Lou."

"To tell you the truth, Ar'minta," said Samuel slowly, "I ain't a-going to be comfortable with that poor kid. Did you see how she looked at us?"

"And never a tear for my big Lou, only over them old dresses."

"There, there, Mother!"

She gave a laugh which was half a sob. "Maybe they was worth crying over at that . . . Lou used to dress her right nice, so fresh and pretty. Maybe she'll tell us what she's been through and maybe she won't. I never did like that Ellen Payson."

"That ain't your trouble, and you know it, Ar'-minta. You seen how the kid looked around, like she was too good for us all. You're one as needs to be loved."

"She used to be right cute. Lou spoiled her with all those fine-lady ways; but then she was the only one. She ain't cute now."

"That she ain't."

"Cambridge ain't what Lou wanted for her, Sam'l, nor yet Jim didn't neither. They does a grade a year in them Baltimore schools, not half a grade like here. Lou told me so. Right proud she was of Minty Lou's education."

"Well, look here," Samuel said, summing up, "it ain't no question of whether Minty Lou likes it with us or what Lou wanted. She's our grand-child and Lou's kid. She's got a place that's her own and no one else's. She ain't got her druthers, nor we ain't got ours neither. If she don't care for Cambridge, she can go off the way Lou did when she's sixteen."

"She belongs to us," Araminta agreed, her voice growing more cheerful. "I'm still her Grandma Minty, and she's my little Lou, whatever she is . . . my poor little Lou."

"I *shall* go off when I'm sixteen," argued Minty Lou to herself. "I won't like it here, not even if they want me to." But Grandpa had said this was

where she belonged, and Grandma had agreed. They had found a bed for her and a chair at the table. Grandma was taking up the hems of her dresses. This was her place, and it would have to do till she was sixteen.

"It's on my mind now," Grandma was saying, "That there was something I wished I'd told Lou while I had the chance. Up there in Baltimore, Sam'l, folks don't pay much mind to other folks; and Lou didn't neither, not always. Maybe I didn't care too much for the city, but I was real proud of Lou; and I might've said something which come to me there if I hadn't been sort of angry. I might've said as how it was her who ought to have been named for Minty Tubman and not me. She'd've liked that."

"It don't matter too much about the name," said Samuel gently. "She was our Lou, and she wan't like nobody else in the wide world. I guess she knew that."

They were silent for such a long time that Minty Lou got tired of listening and went back to bed. She lay there for a little while, warm and sleepy, remembering Momma.

Grandma Minty came up to get in beside Marybelle, but before she did so, she hung up Minty Lou's dress, shortened ready for the morning. Then she stroked her head to feel if it were hot and straightened the pillow. Something dropped out of Minty Lou's hand onto the floor with a little clatter. In the light of the candle which she had brought up, Grandma Minty saw that it was a chipped badge of white enamel with S for supervisor on it in red. She put it gently by the limp hand on the pillow. Then she blew out the candle and climbed into bed, weeping silently for her big Lou.